The Merchant Adventurer

Patrick E McLean

The Merchant Adventurer

Patrick E McLean

This book is for sale at http://www.amazon.com

This version was published on 2014-01-11

ISBN 978-1492973522

Tweet This Book!

Please help Patrick E McLean by spreading the word about this book on Twitter!

The suggested hashtag for this book is #MerchantAdventurer.

Find out what other people are saying about the book by clicking on this link to search for this hashtag on Twitter:

https://twitter.com/search?q=#MerchantAdventurer

Contents

Accolades

(for How to Succeed in Evil)

Well written and a wonderful twist on a well-heeled trope. Thank you Mr. McLean for a great deal of laughs and a thought provoking book: what is the ultimate use/abuse of power and who is responsible?

David Willis

Truly Hilarious. It is so difficult to find truly funny novels, but this book definitely is one of the best. If you like the "frustrated anti-hero" archetype, then you will love Edwin Windsor. Basil Fawlty as a consultant to supervillians.

Darryl Lashambe

Normally funny books make me chuckle and that's about it. This book is the first book since 'Good Omens' to make me laugh so hard that I lost my place and then prevented me from reading further by putting tears in my eyes.

If you love superheroes and comics like I do, or hate them like my wife does, you'll find this book awesome.

Adam Haner

Brimming with anarchic wit, this book is a refreshingly original antidote to the reams of identikit superhero stories that have marched across our pages and screens over the last few years.

Glenn Murphy

"Nobody offers the hilarious car-crash of ideas that McLean does. At once zany and thoughtful. His writing is as much a map of the human condition as it is satire."

– John F. Roberts

What? No, I haven't read it. I'm too busy reviewing pain-in-the-ass novels that fall into the same tired-old genres that we've been pushing for years. That, and I could never actually admit to reading *genre fiction* you see. No, no. Another shovelful of dull tombs about dysfunctional American families for me, if you please.

That guy who snubbed Patrick at the New York Times Review of Books.

Introduction

In the middle of my life, I found myself in a maze of twisting passages, each alike...

I've had this thing I've needed to get out of my system. It's writing a heroic tale without a hero in it. How to Succeed in Evil, my first book, is about a really smart guy in a world of superpowered people. He succeeds not because he's powerful, but because he's smart, ruthless and (in a very strange way) reasonable. The book you hold in your hands (or file you hold on your digital device) represents another one of those stories. And it had an odd genesis.

I begged my way into a gig writing and designing levels for an cRPG (computer role playing game). This is not the kind of thing I would be likely to do, except that it was the sequel to Wasteland, a game which my 16 year-old self deeply adored and admired. So of course, I helped fund the Kickstarter for Wasteland 2. Since I knew one of the original designers, Mike Stackpole, I asked him if I could pitch in some words. I was happy to do so for free as a favor to my 16-year-old testosterone-addled self for not getting me killed at that awkward age. I was not suicidal, but curiosity and fearlessness are dangerous brew.

I did some concept stuff for Wasteland 2. I came up with some ideas and mythology for the cults in the game as well as some background bits. Brian Fargo liked it, so he asked me to do more. He and Matt Findley were very patient and helpful as they coached me through the process of writing and designing levels. Along the way I got to meet and work with very talented and dedicated people including Chris Avellone, Colin McComb, Nathan Long, Chris Keenan and iv

Kevin Saunders.

I learned a great deal from the experience. And I discovered something interesting about myself along the way. I knew a lot more about computer role playing games than I realized. In fact, I had played most all of the seminal games in the genre. Misspent youth? Perhaps.

Enter the Merchant

One of my most favorite, and one of the most ancient games was the original Wizardry. Wizardry and Ultima came out at, effectively, the same time and they have served to define the cRPG genre ever since. Wizardry gave the first (albeit crude) first-person perspective I ever encountered in a game. Ultima used the top-down perspective that would one day evolve to frazzle my nerves in Starcraft.

I played Wizardry on an Apple III. This was the same box on which I learned to program Pascal. This ungainly beige wonder was also connected to my first hard drive. A 10 pound miracle of innovation called the Apple ProFile. Who would ever use more than 5 megs anyway?

Thirty-two years later, I drew on the experience of playing Wizardry and countless other games, to write Wasteland 2. And that's when I remembered Boltac.

Just as Wizardry is the granddaddy of all cRPGs. Boltac is the granddaddy of all merchants and stores in cRPGs. For me he was a magnificent bastard of a character. In spite of having no in-game characterization at all. In fact, the only hint you got about him was a note in the manual suggesting that he would sell you his arms. This ambiguity was intentional.

Oh, and there was one other thing you quickly learned about Boltac – his absolutely ruthless approach to trade. Boltac's Trading Post was quite literally the only game in town. And he perfectly exploited his monopoly privilege in a way that would make the greediest inside trader say, "Damn, dude. That's harsh."

In economic terms, he knew exactly how much everything was worth and exactly what to sell it for to get the most money. This is something that business people would give their *eyeteeth* to know. Perfect information does not exist. And the whole of useful, durable knowledge about pricing can be summed up in the phrase, "Whatever the traffic will bear." The only way to know that is to make a deal and try to find out. But you're always, always wrong. The only question is "by how much?"

If you've ever negotiated a salary or a project payment or the purchase of a ruby necklace, then you'll know that feeling – that awful feeling that you might have left money on the table. But that's the thing with Boltac. He *never* left money on the table. And he never lost a sale because he asked for too much.

What would a story about that guy be like?

This question popped into my head as I was writing the dialog for a merchant in Wasteland 2. Balcom Maldrige, the merchant you can find in the Free-Trade Zone in the Gipper's area of Los Angeles. The idea of the groups of people you encounter in WL2 is that, in response to the physic terror of the end of the world, they grouped themselves into cults created around one aspect of pre-war society. With the Gippers it was Ronald Reagan.

Playing a game, especially one with as rich, dark and satirical a subtext as Wasteland 2, it's easy to overlook the process of writing any character in any setting. Among the questions that the writer has to ask is "What does the world/scenario look like to this character?" Often the world is fanciful, absurd and ridiculous. This presents no problem as long as the creator(s) maintain an internal consistency.

So what does the world of a fantasy RPG look like to a merchant like Boltac?

In Wizardry, you don't have to answer this question. He's just the store, he never talks or interacts with the players. But now, countless cRPG's in, we need an answer to questions like this to refresh the genre.

So here are the facts of the Merchant's existence as I see them.

1. He's trying to make a buck.
2. He sells to penniless, unsuccessful adventurers who are trying to stop some malevolent blight (evil wizard, dragon, ancient demon, what-have-you) they believe has plagued the land.
3. Most of these unsuccessful adventurers get killed.
4. The Malevolent Blight might not actually be a plague on the land. (Maybe it's just misunderstood? Maybe it's all a con?)
5. The ones who come back from their adventures do so with loot that they want to sell.
6. The merchant then, would be a surly, jaded pawnbroker, making his living off a desperate, deluded and non-productive group of people.
7. He's a greedy bastard who sticks his neck out for nobody.

So then the question became, how do you tell a story where the merchant is driven to become the hero and save the day? Piece of cake. En-henh. But whatever. The book that follows is the result. I unapologetically wrote this story for myself. But you're certainly welcome to enjoy it too.

1

"I am the Chosen One. Only I can bring peace and restore balance to the land," said the blonde Knight in Shining™ Armor.

"You still don't understand," said the Ranger, clad in mail. He hiked up his sleeve and showed the mark that was burned into his arm. "This symbol of the Cruel God Azaz signifies–"

"Azaz my Az-ass! That signifies your whore of a mother spilled bacon fat on you when you were a child."

The men drew swords and faced off. But before either of them could swing, a thin man dressed in a faded black cloak stepped between them. He said, "Please, my Lords, please! We mustn't fight amongst ourselves."

"Out of my way, Rattick! You are but a hireling!" cried the Ranger. He waved a gauntleted fist in Rattick's pinched face. "It is my destiny to run him through."

"Your destiny? Don't be absurd. I am the CHOSEN ONE!" shrieked the Knight.

"Perhaps," said Rattick, "you have both been Chosen." They stopped to consider this possibility. Rattick pressed on, "We go to face a mighty foe. A powerful Wizard in a deep dungeon. Perhaps all the others have failed not because they didn't have *a* Chosen One, but because they didn't have *enough* Chosen Ones."

"I AM THE CHOSEN ONE!" they both shouted.

Okay, thought Rattick, that was a mistake. Best to let the morons fight it out. But before he could step off the field of idiocy, the Enchantress chimed in. "Don't talk to him like that," she said. "He is a member of this party. Moreover, the sacred vows I have taken at the Shrine of Lauranda mean that I must treat all beings with courtesy and respect, and eat nothing that has a face," she intoned with reverence.

To Rattick's surprise, this worked. The men lowered their swords and apologized (apologized!) to each other. Rattick stared longingly at the Enchantress. She was beautiful. Her curves were accentuated by the belt of gold rings that encircled her hips and the massive ruby that gleamed from between her breasts. Perhaps there was a way he could... No. Better not to think of such things.

"Forgive me, good Rattick," said the Knight, his head bowed. "Though it is true that we have hired you to guide us to the lair of foul Wizard Dimsbury, you have served us true and are a member of this party."

"We brave Companions," said the Ranger, "we happy few, each, in our own way, fulfilling a mystical and wondrous destiny. Yes, we are all sorry to have used you so badly, faithful Rattick."

Rattick's jaw dropped. Could they be serious? Was it possible that they were they conning him rather than the other way around? He clacked his teeth together and pasted a smile across his sour mouth. "Not at all, good sirs," said Rattick. "We are Adventurers! Spirits run high with ones so bold as we."

"Huzzah!" cried the Knight, as he lifted his heavy blade in the air.

"Huzzah!" cried the Ranger, clanging his blade against the sword of the man he was very recently going to run through.

"Huzzah," giggled the Enchantress, clapping her hands together and sending a tiny fireball up to dance against the blades.

"You gotta be kidding," thought Rattick as he lifted his dagger in half-hearted salute.

• • •

A few hours later, they emerged from the forest into a strange clearing and Rattick announced, "This is it."

"What do you mean?" asked the Ranger. "You mean this? It's just a door in the side of a hill." And so it was. A frame and stout oak door had been incongruously installed into the side of a well-grassed mound perhaps 25 feet high and 50 feet around. In front of the door was a reed mat that read "Go Away."

"You expected a sign?" asked Rattick.

"Well, I... I don't know what I expected," said the Ranger

"That's why you hired me to be your guide."

"No, good fellow," protested the Ranger, "do not wound me so. You are no longer hireling, but boon Companion, a full member of our brave band."

"Yes, yes," said Rattick, "let us to it, boon Companions." He reached for the door but before he could open it, the Enchantress interrupted.

"Stop! We must first seek the benediction of Lauranda. Her blessing will keep us safe during our time of trial."

The Knight and the Ranger both drew their swords and knelt. Rattick rolled his eyes. Just get it over with. He didn't know how much more amateur hour he could take. But he consoled himself with the knowledge that it would all be over soon.

The Enchantress completed her babbling, and they ventured into the Wizard's lair. It did not take long before the Companions heard rumblings and gnashings of teeth from the darkness ahead. Rattick smiled. The Troll was still there, and he sounded hungry. "Stay here, faithful Companions," he said, playing it for all it was worth, "I will use my mastery of stealth and shadow to scout the way."

He handed his torch to the Ranger. He took two steps forward into the darkness of the cave. With a flourish, he wrapped his cape of faded black around him and vanished. Rattick heard his boon Companions gasp as he disappeared.

"Oh, he's very good," said the Enchantress.

Rattick was good, but so were his tools. The cape, mean and worn as it looked, was a powerful Magical item. It possessed three properties that Rattick knew of. One: when closed, it imposed upon all who saw it a powerful desire to look elsewhere. Two: in anything from darkness to light shadow, it rendered the user invisible. Three: it was an item so enchanted as to be nearly impossible to steal from its rightful owner. Rattick had learned this the hard way, procuring this wonderful item only after killing its previous rightful owner.

"Be thankful he did not charge us more," muttered the Knight.

Again Rattick smiled at the nothingness of the dark. The bill for Rattick's services was about to come due, and the brave-but-stupid Knight would find it held many hidden charges. Rattick took a few steps around the corner and squatted in the passageway. Faithful Companions? How could they fall for that? Rattick wasn't sticking his neck out any farther than he had to. He waited for a time, then unwrapped his cloak and returned to the pool of torchlight in which his brave, faithful, and gullible Companions waited.

As he stepped into the light, he donned an expression of fear. With a skill long practiced, he trembled as he spoke. "It is a *Troll* my Companions. A creature most large and fearsome. I fear it is more than we can defeat. We should turn back."

"Ha ha ha ha!" laughed the Knight, taking the bait. "A Troll! That is nothing to a Knight of the Yarven Dawn."

"And it is even less to the Blessed and Chosen of Azaz," said the Ranger, revealing the strange mark branded on his arm for what felt like the thousandth time.

Rattick swallowed his disgust and said, "You are so much braver and stronger than I."

The Knight drew his sword and said, "Stay behind me and learn how it is done. Fear not, Rattick, for you are in the company of Heroes."

"I shall not let you steal the Glory!" cried the Ranger as he shouldered the Knight aside.

Rattick couldn't believe it – the idiots charged! A frontal assault on a Troll? They were so stupid it was a wonder they could remember to breathe.

The Enchantress edged past him, smelling of exotic perfume. "I will see if I can bind the creature with The Mother's Embrace. Stay behind me, and you will be safe."

He followed her swaying hips through the corridor, for once grateful for torchlight. There was a roar and the stench of something awful. Rattick knew this to be the Troll's breath. Nothing smells worse than rotting flesh trapped between Troll teeth.

When she saw the Troll, the Enchantress raised her arms and began casting a spell. As her hands wove their intricate pattern, Rattick slid his knife across her perfect, white throat. She gasped as her life's blood poured down her neck, over the exquisite ruby necklace and into the deep valley of her heaving breasts. Before she could make another sound, Rattick covered her mouth and dragged her into the darkness.

She whimpered softly and grew weak. Rattick set her against the wall and removed his hand from her face. When he lifted her chin she mouthed the word, "Why?" Rattick bent down and kissed the dying woman on the lips. Her eyes fluttered as her life left the husk of her body.

Rattick tore the necklace from her throat. Then he wiped the blood from it with a black silk handkerchief. In the distance, the screams of the Chosen Ones ended in a terrible, squishy, bone-crunching noises.

Staring into the glittering facets of the ruby, Rattick answered the dead woman. "Why? Because it was a kindness. Because there are worse things in the depths of this dungeon than you can imagine. Because this is what happens when you choose to play a dangerous game. All of those are close, but if you really want the truth of it..." He looked up and saw that she was dead. "Because I can."

2

Rattick threw the necklace on the oak counter and watched the light dance in it like a living thing. He nodded at it and asked, "Have you ever seen such exquisite workmanship?"

Boltac, the Merchant on the other side of the counter, picked up the ruby necklace and examined it closely. He gave Rattick a hard look and frowned. Maybe the deal was good, but this shifty-eyed, greasy-hair scavenger looked like he would pick his own pocket if he thought he could get away with it.

Boltac's eyes were swathed in a soft round face, but they were sharp enough that Rattick would not brave his gaze. And despite the fleshiness that middle age had added to Boltac's neck and gut, his jaw had stayed strong and block-like. He was not a man that people easily got the better of.

Boltac studied the necklace for a while. Then he licked his thumb, rubbed the necklace's setting, and muttered, "You missed a spot."

"Missed a spot?" asked Rattick, as smooth as water over river rock.

"Blood, Rattick. There's some blood left on this necklace."

Rattick shrugged. "Probably mine. I try to use stealth, but the Orc I took it from put up quite a fight."

"En-henh," Boltac said as ran his hand across his shaven pate. "Not that I want to know, but what is an Orc?"

"A fearsome new creature wreaking havoc on the good people of Robrecht."

"En-henh," said Boltac, not buying it. "And you, uh, count yourself among those good people?"

"Of course. I am no mighty Hero, like some, but I do what little I can."

"Okay, Rattick, I'm gonna make you an offer on your necklace here. The setting is crap, but the stone is very nice. But before I do – not for nuttin' but, Orcs? You're shittin' me, right?"

"Oh no, stout Merchant, I assure you, Orcs are very real."

"Really? Kobolds, I heard of. Trolls, I heard of. Dragons, sure, but Orcs? C'mon. What does an Orc look like?"

"Gentle Merchant, I hope that you never see one, but I assure you, if you do, you will know it for the Orc that it is."

"En-henh."

"Let me tell you the fearsome tale of how I came to acquire this necklace and then perhaps you will better understand the threat that the fearsome Orc–"

"You can spare me the story, Rattick," said Boltac.

"You don't enjoy Tales of Valor?" asked Rattick with a smile.

"Tales of Valor? No. I enjoy tales of profit."

"I don't know any sagas that involve tales of profit," said Rattick. "But Tales of Valor, of great daring... the bards sing many songs of those."

"Yeah, I don't really care for singing either. In fact, let's just cut all the bullshit. I'm pretty sure I know how you got this."

"Yessssss," purred Rattick, running his finger over the ruby, "but do you care?"

"Not if you'll take fifteen gold for it I don't."

"Fifteen gold? I risked my neck for this!"

"Your neck? I'm pretty sure *you* risked somebody *else's* neck for this particular bauble. Fine, seventeen for the gem, and two gold for the rest of it." Boltac said, indicating the pile of equipment on the floor.

"But this sword almost defeated a Troll!"

"Yeah, and it almost doesn't have that huge nick in it. And why does everything in that pile smell like Troll shit?"

They haggled like this for a while, and settled on a price of 22 gold for the lot. When Rattick left, Boltac muttered a curse and had to work to keep from spitting on his own floor.

He placed the ruby in one of three lockboxes behind the counter and then dragged the bundle of equipment into the back to see how badly he had been taken. The sword was of higher quality than he had hoped for, and there were a number of items that, while they wouldn't fetch top price, would provide good use. The odd piece of armor, some leather goods. He threw out a badly damaged boot and debated opening a nondescript fabric sack. Sacks could be trouble. For that matter so could gems.

He grunted as he stood up. He trudged wearily back to the front of the store. From beneath the counter, he produced a brass-tipped wand that was clipped to the underside of the thick oak. He took the wand to the back and guided it carefully over all the items.

The wand did not grow warm or shriek or vibrate or do any of the many colorful and destructive things it did in the presence of Magic. The wand was not merely a Magic wand. It was a Magic *detecting* wand. Very rare, very expensive. But, for a man who dealt in items of unknown origins purchased from characters of questionable virtue, it was indispensable.

"Ennh," grunted Boltac, more relieved than disappointed. Boltac hated Magic. It wasn't just dangerous, it was bad for business. When a customer couldn't try on a pair of gloves for fear that they would turn out to be MaGrief's Gauntlets of Self-Abuse, business suffered.

That's why he kept the wand secreted under his the counter. Pick up a cursed ruby necklace and there was no telling what might happen. Before he had procured his wand, Boltac had spent six months with a cursed Goblet of Thirst stuck to his hand. As annoying as that was, that wasn't the worst part of the curse. When liquid was poured into the Goblet, it heated up and burned the hand that held it.

He rubbed the scarred flesh of his left hand. Ugh, Magic. It seemed like it should be useful but its power always seemed to go awry. Maybe it was fate. Maybe it was karma. Maybe it was that Wizards had a particularly cruel and ironic sense of humor. Whatever the reason, Boltac was certain that the world would be better off without Magic. But there was nothing to be done about it. People may revile a Merchant but, in the end, a Merchant can only sell what the people want.

He pulled on a stout thong he wore around his neck and, with a jingle, a cluster of charms, tokens, and amulets emerged from beneath his tunic. He pawed at them for a while until he came to an odd one cast in bronze. It was a small statue of one bull mounting another. The customary token of Dallios, Lord of the Deal. Dallios was a Southron God, little known in cold Robrecht, but when it came to religions, Boltac didn't discriminate. Boltac was a superstitious man, but he prided himself on being able to make a deal with anybody.

He kissed the Bull with Two Backs and muttered a prayer of thanks to Dallios that, this time at least, he hadn't been the bull on the bottom.

Just then the front door clattered against its crude copper bell. A customer! The Lord of the Deal smiled on Boltac today, and he hurried to see what fresh profit Dallios had seen fit to bring him.

3

At the front of the store, Boltac found a strapping young lad, a Farm Boy no doubt, staring at a rack of swords with an open mouth. The boy was so entranced by the cold and lethal steel on the wall that he didn't even turn when Boltac entered the room. Boltac stepped behind the counter like a captain stepping on the deck of his ship. "Can I help you?"

"I need a sword," said the Farm Boy, his eyes not leaving the weaponry.

"Then you have come to the right place. Welcome, my young friend, to Boltac's General Store and Dungeon Outfittery. We have everything that a strapping young Adventurer like yourself could need to loot your way to Fame and Glory."

"We?" asked the lad, with the kind of innocence that can only come from hard work, clean living, and getting kicked in the head by livestock.

"Yes, the Royal We. Or, in this case, the Shopkeeper's We."

"But there is only one of you?"

"Yes, but I am so eager to help you, I will work as hard as two men. Now, what's the story? Who you gotta stab? Who you gonna loot?"

"No," said the Farm Boy as he hung his head in embarrassment. "It's not like that. I don't want to loot anybody. I... I just have to... I mean, I am about to embark on an Adventure of High Purpose and Consequence." With this last phrase, Boltac's hopes rose. Maybe the kid was a little slow, but those fancy words sounded like money to Boltac. He smiled like a fleshy shark.

"My friend, you have come to the right place. High Purpose and Consequence is what we are all about at Boltac's. Why, the Duke of Robrecht himself has granted me my license to purvey. He has an eye to quality, his Dukeship does, and his warrant of commerce personally guarantees that this,"–he indicated his dark, dusty store with an expansive gesture of his hands–"is the finest merchandise you can buy in the town of Robrecht."

"But, yours is the only store the Duke allows in the town of Robrecht."

"Yes, I see that you are a quick study," said Boltac, directing the young man back through the shelves. "I invite you to direct your keen wit toward my wares. Here we have an assortment of torches and oil-bearing devices. If you notice this one–with the curved blade on the handle–particularly good if you are surprised coming around a corner."

Boltac turned the Farm Boy sharply and indicated a floor-to-ceiling rack of glass bottles, "Here, of course, we have our major and minor healing potions–antidotes, ointments, and unguents of all kinds. A must for any prudent Adventurer. These potions are brewed by the finest Mercian apothecaries and brought in by mule train once a moon."

Moving right along, Boltac directed his young shopper towards the racks in the back, "And here is the armor. A must for all but barbarians and the most self-confident Magic workers. You aren't a Magic worker are you?"

"I don't think so," said the lad, a little overwhelmed by how fast this was all coming at him.

"Perfect, then you have your choice of chain mail, splint mail, ring mail, plate mail, plate armor and–far less protection but the girls love it–leather armor. Feel that? Very supple."

"But what I need is a sword," protested the Farm Boy.

"En-henh," said Boltac, "Which brings us to back to lighting. A question of prominent importance to any Adventurer."

The Farm Boy looked longingly back at the swords.

"I know, I know," continued Boltac, "you think the thing with the pointy end is the most important bit of gear you can buy."

"A Hero's life depends on the strength of his blade."

"Sometimes. But there are two things I can *guarantee* you are going to need. 1) Water. 2) Light."

"What about food?"

"Eh, you can live for days without food. A strong lad like you could eat what he kills, but without water... not so much. And the dark. Are you comfortable in the dark?"

"I have walked this land at night since I was a small child."

"And now that you're a big child... I'm sorry, I'm sorry, I'm just having fun. My point here is, you know what lives far, far underground, in the darkness?"

"I do not, but I am ready to boldly face the unknown."

"En-henh. You got no idea. For that matter, neither do I. But what I *do* know is that whatever horrible underground thing you mean to bash to a pulp in the name of your personal fame or fortune, you can bet that *it* can see in the dark."

The Farm Boy stood there with a brave, stupid look on his face.

"And you know what can't see in the dark?"

"Uh..."

"You. You can't see in the dark. Can you?"

"No."

"Then trust me, you pain-in-the-ass, take a lantern. In fact, take two and some torches, just in case."

"What about that one," the Farm Boy asked, pointing to a lamp that hung on its own peg high on the wall.

"Oh, that, you have a very good eye, my friend. That is the Magic Lantern of Lamptopolis. It cannot be broken and it never goes out as long as it's carried."

"Lamptopolis?" asked the Farm Boy.

"Okay, you caught me, I made it up. But it's a lantern and it's clearly Magic."

"It's beautiful. How does it work?"

"It's Maaaaaaaaagic. That's how it works. Some kinda glowing crystal in the center there. You pick it up, it turns on. But trust me, it can't be broken."

"How do you know that?"

"You've never had apprentices, have you? Third rule of shopkeeping: If a thing can't be broken by an apprentice, it can't be broken. Now lemme see here. It's got an inscription on it..."

Boltac wrangled a stepladder over to the wall and lifted the lamp from its resting place. As soon as he touched its handle, the crystal in the center of the lamp flickered to life. "Yeah," Boltac said, rubbing the dust from the letters that were cut into the bottom of the Lantern's base. "It says, 'Burns with the Flame of a True Heart.' Well, it's not much of a flame, is it? But at least you don't have to carry oil for it."

He handed the Lantern to the Farm Boy. As soon as the boy touched the handle, the Lantern blazed with a brilliant light; so bright, Boltac realized it had been a long, long time since he had cleaned the store. He closed his eyes to stop the pain.

"Wow," said the Farm Boy.

"Give me that," snapped Boltac, snatching the Lantern from the boy's hand. The lamplight returned to a dull flicker.

"How much is it?"

"More than you can afford," Boltac grumbled as he hung the Lantern back on the peg.

"That's okay," said the Farm Boy in a fresh-faced and agreeable way that made Boltac hate him all the more, "what I really need is a sword."

"Maybe you do and maybe you don't. Keep an open mind for me. We've got pikes, bows, warhammers, battle axes, halberds, flails, morningstars, maces and the largest selection of fine daggers this side of the mountains."

"I don't want a mace. I want a sword."

"Of course you do. And once again, Boltac's has you covered! We've got short swords, long swords, broadswords, rapiers, cutlasses, sabers, scimitars, shishkas, slabas–did I mention, the finest selection of daggers of quality this side of the mountains? While it's true that most of our blades have never been tested in battle, this is in keeping with our philosophy of passing the savings and the Glory on to you."

"Well, uh, I'm afraid..."

"Afraid? A big, strapping lad like you? Don't be ridiculous. Why, after you've been properly outfitted by Uncle Boltac, you'll have nothing to fear in this world. You'll be able to take on a Dragon with one hand and an OwlBear with the other. And therein lies the value of quality equipment."

"No, it's just that I'm afraid those beautiful swords,"–his eyes grew wide as he looked at them–"are all too expensive for me."

The smile drained from Boltac's face, but he continued as if he hadn't just been kicked in the wallet. "Don't be silly. At Boltac's, we have equipment to fit every budget." He kicked a bucket of swords that sat next the counter. "Have a look at our discount bucket."

The Farm Boy pulled a sword from the bucket and then dropped it back in quickly. "This sword still has blood on it!"

"That's how you know it works! A gold piece gets you the pick of the barrel."

"A gold piece?" said the lad, looking concerned.

"Well," said Boltac, who was starting to get a very bad feeling about the entire transaction, "At Boltac's there's always room to negotiate. But try a few; see how you like the balance and whatnot."

"I've been trying to save money to buy a sword, sir. Scrounging for herbs, seeing if anyone needs rats killed. But no one needs rats killed. And the countryside is bare for miles around..." He trailed off.

Boltac nodded knowingly. The only vermin that plagued Robrecht was an infestation of down-on-their-luck Adventurers. "I understand how it is. And how much did you say you have been able to save?"

"Not enough, I'm afraid. So I was wondering if I could rent a sword."

"RENT A SWORD?" Boltac shouted. "Do you not see the sign?" he asked, pointing at the sign that clearly read, "All Sales Final."

"I can't read, sir."

"Oh, of course not."

"Please sir, it's so I can rescue the Love of my Life. She was taken, you see. Abducted by Scoundrels."

"Oh, well, that changes everything," said Boltac, as his face grew hard. "Tell me more?" he asked, as if it were a dare.

"Well, sir, she is a Priestess of Dar. And, well..."

"Aren't they supposed to be virgins? Those Priestesses of Dar?"

The young man blushed and said, "It's more of a suggestion than a rule, sir. If you know what I mean." His face grew serious. "But if it helps, *I* was a virgin."

"Help? How would that help?"

"She's gone and got herself into trouble. I've gotten word from a friend that she's being held in a tower and requires a Hero to rescue her."

"So what's keeping this broad from walking outta that tower herself?"

"Broad? Sir, you speak of the Love of my Life–"

"No offense, but your life hasn't been that long yet."

"–and she's been placed at the top of the tower and sleeps a deathless sleep under an Evil Spell."

"En-henh. That's a Sleeping Beauty, kid," Boltac said. He was about to explain that the Sleeping Beauty was the name of a con game– popular among some of Robrecht's less-than-upstanding citizens– whereby a young man was seduced, lured into a trap, and relieved of any valuable items he might have. Like, for instance, a borrowed sword. But the Farm Boy had bolted from the barn, and Boltac could see that there was no catching him.

"Yes, she is a *real* beauty, sir. Asleep or awake. I knew you would understand. So, if I had a sword, I could go and rescue her. And there would certainly be Treasure after I defeated the monsters that have been set to protect her from all but the bravest and most faithful Hero. Understand, I have no care for this Treasure. Only my lady Love. So all the valuables would be yours. All that for loaning me a sword."

Boltac winced under the onslaught of the boy's sincerity. "But just a sword? I mean, armor would help too, right?"

"Yes, it would, but..."

"And some healing potions, you know, just to be safe."

"Well, of course, but..."

"And perhaps a flying steed. White, with large flapping wings."

"You have a flying steed?" the boy asked in awe.

"Even if I did, you couldn't afford it."

"But, we're talking about a loan."

"No, *you're* talking about a loan. I'm sorry, you're just gonna have to find yourself another Priestess of Eternally Questionable Virtue, kid."

"Look, I'm not asking for armor or a flying horse, I'm just asking to borrow a sword."

Boltac looked the boy dead in the eyes and said, "I'm not giving you any discounts."

"It's not a discount. It's a loan."

"It's the worst kind of discount. It's a 100% discount!"

"But I'd bring it back. Maybe with a few nicks, but definitely covered in Glory."

"Oh, Glory is it? Would that enhance the retail value?"

"Yes, yes," he said eagerly, unaware of the trap he was falling into.

"Because you are such a great fighter."

"Yes, that's it."

"Powerful, strong," Boltac prompted.

"Yes."

"Ready for danger from any quarter."

"I might not look like much, sir, but I'll be a mighty Hero yet."

"All you need is a sword? Is that right?"

"Yes, please, sir. Please. Haven't you ever been young and in Love?"

Boltac's face soured. "I was never young. Look, kid, I'm not going to loan you a sword. But I do have an old mace I keep behind the counter, you know, in case of trouble. It's not much to look at, but it's always been lucky for me. I like to think it would be good luck for you. Would you like to see it?"

"Very much."

Boltac lifted the mace up from behind the counter. As he raised the weapon high in the air, the lad's trusting, cow-like eyes followed it, studying every detail of the well-worn wood, the wrapped leather handle, and the business end studded with heavy iron nails. Boltac saw the lad move from disappointment to hope. "Yes," his eyes seemed to say, "a mace. I could do it with a mace."

Boltac hit him right between the eyes and knocked him out cold.

4

In the center of Robrecht, there was a river. In the center of this river was an island. And in the center of this island was a very damp castle. And in the very damp center of this very damp castle was a Duke on a throne. Both of which were also damp. And one of them was terribly bored.

The Duke started what would have been a mighty yawn, but he quickly worked to stifle it. This resulted in one of his eyes closing and his mouth attempting to wrap itself around his strong nose. When his face was not in spasm, the Duke came close enough to being noble. He had a finely drawn face, thick dark hair, and a nose well-suited for looking down at people. But if you looked in his eyes, the effect of a cruel Mercian conqueror would have been spoiled. With more force of personality, his eyes might have been piercing. But alas, from the loins of the most powerful Empire on Earth had sprung another stuffed personage with weak chin and sunken eyes.

He was yawning because he was holding court. Well, such as court as could be held in the remote and unimpressive Duchy of Robrecht to which he had been consigned. There were no glittering courtiers here. There were no ladies-in-waiting. There was just the Duke, an uncomfortable wooden chair and a long line of disputes that the Duke was expected to settle before he would be allowed to go to his supper.

"Messrs Rudolph and Fuad, herders of goats!" the Chamberlain announced. The Duke waved his hand and the men were brought before him.

"He had advantage of my goat, my Lord. And I desire compensation," said a cross-eyed man as he glared in the general direction of the man standing next to him. The Duke turned his gaze at the accused, a man wearing a goat-skin helmet. Was the helmet this man's idea of formal dress? the Duke wondered. The Duke opened his mouth to ask, but then thought better of it. He squinted at the man and tried to decipher the matter on his own.

The pause stretched to such a length that the Chamberlain gently prompted, "My Lord?"

"Advantage?" asked the Duke, unable, with his formal, courtly up-bringing, to understand how having a goat might be an advantage. It was not that there were no goats in the Mercian Empire. It was that his entire life had been carefully constructed to insulate him from all creatures shaggy and uncultured.

"He had knowledge of my best nanny goat."

"Knowledge? I don't understand, of course he has knowledge of your animal," the Duke said, glancing at the dull-eyed, leather-helmeted man who was being accused of bestiality, "He is a fellow goatherd, is he not?"

"No, my Lord," said the cross-eyed man, blushing with the weight of what he must now make painfully obvious. "He..." and then he thrust his pelvis forward and backwards in an unmistakable, rhythmic motion.

"Oh. Oh? OH!" said the Duke, as the facts of the case came into disgusting focus for him. "Really?" He turned to Leather Helmet. "What was it like?"

The Chamberlain began to cough. This was a prearranged signal between the two of them that the Duke was wandering dangerously off course. The Chamberlain did a lot of coughing in the perfor-mance of his duties.

"Very well," the Duke said, "I command you to violate one of *his* sheep."

"WHAT!"

"Yes, yes, my good man; that is justice. He has had one of yours, so, "–the Duke slapped his knee decisively–"you must have one of his. An eye for an eye and an ewe for an ewe. Yes, that certainly has the ring of justice to it, doesn't it? Symmetry and suchlike," the Duke said, feeling awfully proud of himself. But by the look on the goatherd's face, he could see that his legal acumen was lost on the man.

The Chamberlain continued to cough. The Duke became worried about how he might talk his way out of his ruling without seeming that he was contradicting himself. The Duke was aware, vaguely, that he was not the sharpest arrow in the quiver. But he was straight on one point: The only mortal sin a person in power might truly commit was seeming to contradict himself.

He couldn't understand where he had gone wrong. What taboo had he crossed? It was a perfectly logical verdict. He was a perfectly logical ruler. And why did rulers have to explain themselves to their subjects anyway? Maybe it was just Dukes. He was pretty sure if he were a King he wouldn't have had to explain himself to anyone.

Just as he was thinking that, a Wizard appeared in the Great Hall. And this is not to say he made an entrance. One minute there was an empty space on the cold stone floor and the next, there he stood. Shaven pate, black robes, the large silver torque around his neck only slightly larger than the dark circles under his eyes, strange stains under his fingernails–yes, unmistakably a Wizard. One moment he wasn't there, and the next, he was. The Wizard appeared.

There was a gasp as those in the Great Hall jumped back from the man who had apparated into their midst. Nonplussed, the Chamberlain announced, "A man, appearing from nowhere!"

The Wizard looked at the Chamberlain sharply and hissed, "My name is Alston Dimsbury."

"Dimsbury, a Wizard of Considerable Evil..." the Chamberlain said.

The Wizard's look darkened, and more imaginative people in the crowd believed that they saw flames forming in his eyes.

"...whose reputation is much maligned!" the Chamberlain added diplomatically.

"Yes, enough, that's quite enough," said the Duke. "Wizard, you will simply have to wait your turn."

"Oh," said the Wizard. "Is this inconvenient for you? I *am* sorry. Pray, continue with your amusements. My time is of little consequence." He punctuated his sentence with a wave of his hand that turned the cross-eyed goatherd into a rather lovely brown and white nanny goat. This time, even the Chamberlain gasped in fear.

Fuad, the goatherd in the leather helmet, smiled at the newly-minted goat with an unwholesome gleam in his eye. As he rubbed his hand along the length of rope that held up his trousers, the nanny goat gave up a fearful bleat.

Dimsbury said, "As I was saying, don't let me interrupt."

No one spoke. The only sound was the clacking of the goat's hooves as it wisely made for the exit as fast as its terribly confused legs would carry it.

Exasperated that the crowd still wasn't getting the point, Dimsbury said, "What does it take? Must I strike all of you down with a pillar of flame? Gah. Let me outline it for you. I am a *horrible* man. Dimsbury the Terrible. Master of the arcane arts and elder mysteries, summoner of demons, so on and so forth. Now, go. Flee."

And flee they did. When the oaken door had slammed behind them, Dimsbury and the Duke were the only people left in Robrecht's meager throne room.

"There," said the Wizard, "That's better."

"Hullo, Alston, enjoying yourself?" asked the Duke.

"Quite, Weeveston. I do like to make an entrance."

"I apologize for my subjects," said the Duke, "they are a bit... provincial."

"'Thick' is the word I would have used."

"Would you care for some wine?" asked the Duke, as he draped his leg over the side of his chair and slumped with the false exhaustion that can only come with never having worked a day in one's life.

"I want you to *get out*," said the Wizard.

"Uh? Pardon me?"

"I said, get out. Abdicate. Leave this place and take everyone with you."

"I wish that I could," said the Duke, "I never wanted to come to this damp, grey place to begin with."

"Ah, well there you go," said the Wizard, "I love it when things are easy. Did you say there was wine?"

"Wine? We've got it by the barrelful. And by the bottleful in the cabinet over there. Since you've run off all my servants, subjects, and goat herders, you will have to help yourself. All told, this tower and keep contains more wine than I could drink in three lifetimes. Although the prospect of staying here for three lifetimes," the Duke chuckled as he made a slicing motion across his throat.

"I don't think you understand," said Dimsbury, trying to be reasonable, "this is a courtesy call. What I mean to say is that this request is for your benefit, not mine."

"Steady on, old boy," said the Duke. "I'm on your side. I'm ready to do as you command. You want this Kingdom—well this dismal little Duchy—I say you can have it. Good riddance to fickle mountain weather, thick-ankled peasant girls, and goat-violators of every stripe. But, here's the thing, I can't. The minute I leave my post, my family will know of it. In particular my uncle Torvalds, do you know my uncle Torvalds?"

"Can't say I have had the pleasure," said Dimsbury, fighting back the urge to engulf the Duke in flames with a clap of his hands.

"I have the burden of carrying a great name. Weeveston Prestidigitous RampartLion Toroble the 15th, in fact. And this name means that I am not free do what I would like. I am not free to marry whom I like. I am not free to live where I like. I have been sent here. And if I abdicate, Torvalds Toroble will have me killed. By assassin, or generalship of an army on its way to a glorious lost cause, or perhaps just with a good old-fashioned hunting accident."

"How do you know?" asked Dimsbury, still trying to reason with him.

"It's how he did my father, or tried. Hunting 'accident.' And when dear old Dad survived that, Torvalds sent in his very own doctor to poison the man."

"Damn it," cried Dimsbury, "I'm trying very hard not to be the stereotypical Evil Wizard. But you're just not helping. I don't want to be a stereotype. Don't make me be a stereotype."

"I never suggested that you were," said the Duke, with a look of concern on his face.

"I could have swept in from the east and just taken that mine and cavern system for myself. Killed all the miners, released horrible creatures into the countryside. Right? Could have done that, couldn't I?"

"Yes, Alston, you could have, but I don't feel that you are the kind of–"

"But instead, I bought that mine. Paid gold on the barrel head for it. Didn't I?"

"You did. Please, Alston, what has gotten into you? You are a fine neighbor," said the Duke, trying to tell this powerful and somewhat crazed man what he wanted to hear.

"Yes, I am," Dimsbury said, calming enough to take a healthy gulp of wine. "I am a fine neighbor, but you, and I mean the royal You, Duke Robrecht, are not."

"Ugh, Robrecht as a name. Why, it sounds simply ghastly, doesn't it."

"Your subjects are the ghastly bits. Those little people who infest this land. With their grubbing in the dirt and milking of animals."

"Ah, taxpayers," said the Duke, "Yes, my uncle says I am here to farm them."

"Herd them? Wouldn't herd be the word you're looking for?"

"Yes, I suppose it would be. I am to herd them until tax time. And then I shear them and release them back into the fields."

"It's not your sheep that are the problem. Nor your goats. The problem is the relentless press of Adventurers seeking to steal what they imagine is the vast repository of Treasure stashed in my dungeon."

"You have Treasure, Alston? All this time you've been holding out on me?"

"No, no, heavens no. I mean a little *family* money, but nothing to speak of. I am a Wizard, a researcher into the arcane and terrible forces that undergird all of our lives."

"Sounds rather dull to me."

"Well, it's not for everyone, but my work is *important*. Deucedly important. So much so that I've nearly isolated the source of all Magic in this plane of existence."

"Plane of existence?" asked the Duke, wrinkling his face in confusion.

"Sorry, sorry, don't mean to trouble you with technical terms. The thing is, if I can harness this source–tap into and control the very essence–why, I would be the most powerful and accomplished Mage in the history of the world."

"Prize for that, is there?"

"No, Weeveston, there is not. Power is its own reward."

"Ah, yes, well, you'd have to talk to my uncle about that."

"But not on a hunting trip?"

"Oh, ho ho, quite so. Quite so."

"The point is, I keep getting interrupted in my work by these blasted Adventurers. I can't get anything done. And it's your fault."

"My fault?"

"Yes, the endless stream of mendicants, Adventurers, and ne'er do wells who seek to kill me and deprive me of property. It's Brigandry!Utter lawlessness, that you, as the local authority should but down. They want to become rich Heroes by defeating the Evil Wizard. And by defeat I mean murder and rob. Rapine and pillage writ simple." Here Dimsbury had a thought, "Wait, I'm not *Evil*, am I, Weeveston? I try not to be, but some days, Gods, I just don't know."

"No, of course you are not Evil. I've known you since grammar school. A touch mischievous, perhaps. But Evil? No."

"Oh, thank you for saying so. I do appreciate your honesty," said Dimsbury. "At first, I thought the Adventurers would stop coming. You know, after most of the first few waves of looters fell into my traps or afoul of my pets. But their failure dissuaded no one. They doubled their efforts. And then redoubled them after that!

"Most died on the upper levels, but the few that have managed to penetrate deeper into my stronghold, they've caused real damage. So I have been forced to turn away from my important work to employ spies and turncoats, fashion ever more diabolical traps, and oversee the painful logistics of force management and deployment.

I don't want any of this. It's a constant strain and a distraction from my work. I tell you Weeveston, I am close to a deeper knowledge and understanding of the forces that shape our world than any man has ever had before."

The Duke fixed the Wizard with a look and said, "I know what force shapes our world, and sadly, it is heredity."

But the Wizard was on a roll. "And the power! The limitless power. Only *I* should make this connection with the source, lest this power fall into the hands of some *truly* Evil Wizard. So I'm afraid you simply must go. I see no other way."

The Duke smiled with regret, "I would like nothing better than to comply with your wishes, old friend. But my uncle would have me killed. Even if I did leave, it would do you no good. He would come in force and just take the Kingdom back. And it's not like it would solve your problem. I mean, I can't very well take the sheep with me. Or stop members of the herd from seeking you out and troubling you in your research."

"Yes, Weeveston, I suppose you're right. I just–you know, the long hours of study, the feeling of limitless power at one's fingertips. I just thought there must be some way to solve this problem."

"Of course, old boy. Perfectly understandable. Perhaps I could lend you some of my guards, to help ease the burden. But heaven knows my uncle leaves me precious little enough to staff an army. Really more of a garrison. A bunch of drunks in helmets, honestly."

"Yes, I know, we all have our problems. I'm sorry, Weeveston. I've been an ass. I've barged in unannounced. I've hit your man with Tilhphad's Spell of Transformation. Threatened you with ultimatums. I swear Weeveston, on my mother's grave–the soil of which is indispensable for the making of certain potions–I never wanted to be an *Evil* Wizard. A screeching, fire-throwing caricature of myself. But the world... the world will simply drive a man to it."

"Ah, hmm, yes," said the Duke. "You should meet my Aunt Etheline."

"Torvalds' wife?"

"Oh no, he had her killed long ago. Needlepoint 'accident.' He has something of a penchant for killing relatives. No Etheline is his sister. And compared to him *she* is the *ruthless* one."

"Well, that makes me feel better."

"Better?"

"Yes, I would never do such a thing to my own family."

"Your extended family doesn't own and fight over estates and dominions that cover nearly a third of the known world."

"Perhaps you have a point. But *I* would draw the line at assassinating my own family."

"I do as well," said the Duke with an air of resignation, "but only because I don't have the talent to get away with it."

Dimsbury frowned. "Oh, and I should mention, I've dispatched a raiding party."

"Raiding party, well, that doesn't sound so bad. I mean, it's understandable. Fit of temper and all. "

"Of Orcs," said Dimsbury

"Horks? What are those?"

"They ride wolves, Weeveston. Wolves."

"Well whatever they are, they can't be very large if they are riding wolves."

"They are very large wolves."

"Yes, but what is a Hork?"

"No, no, good fellow, an Orc. No 'h'. They are my latest work. Terrible, terribly murderously bloodthirsty creatures. Stronger and faster than a man. Some cultivars have tusks, other do not. They all have greyish-green skin, *almost* impervious to weapons–if not for the constant interruptions I would have gotten that bit right... Look, it's important that you know how bad I feel about this. Wiping out your entire Kingdom–" at the sound of the word Kingdom, the Duke flinched. "Oh, sorry, sorry, Duchy. Very sorry about that, didn't mean to rub it in. Anyway, I feel terrible about all of this old boy, really I do, but it seems the only way to get the peace I need for my work."

"Well, I understand, you were upset, but it's just a raiding party. Probably do the old town some good. A little raiding. Till up the soil, attract more Adventurers. Rallying to the cry of 'defend good ol' Robrecht!'"

"No, no that's not the point. You see, old boy, I mean to drive you out. Work salt into the earth so nothing will ever grow here again."

"Wait, how many people in this raiding party? I mean how many of these Horks?"

"Orcs"

"...do you have?"

"Oh, a few thousand, by now I should say!"

"Oh, well, why didn't you say so?" exclaimed the Duke, breaking out into a smile.

"What difference does it make?"

"Well if it was two dozen or so, it would be a mere raiding party. But a thousand, perhaps two. Yes, two thousand?"

"I'm a Wizard," said the Wizard, "just not with numbers."

"Well, a quick look at the treasury will reveal that neither am I. But, anything over 500 is clearly an army, right?"

"So?"

"Well, I wouldn't have abdicated, you see. I would have been INVADED!"

"Yes."

"Well, that solves my problem! I just slip away into the night. The warmth of exile in the Southron Kingdoms and the embrace of my wife–"

"Weeveston, you're married?"

"Oh, yes, for ages now. Arranged, but she is pleasant enough, as wives go. But she took one look at this damp tower and left me. She repaired to her father's estates in the south. Something about mold growing in her hair…

"But never mind that now. You have released me old friend. You have released me! I will instruct my household to pack at once."

"Probably for the best. The Orcs should descend on the town shortly after midnight."

"Oh, how very gruesome and terrifying."

"Yes, I thought it a nice touch."

"The only thing, old boy," the Duke said, the smile dropping from his face, "is my uncle. He will take it hard. He will come for revenge."

"No worries, Weeveston. I can handle your Uncle Torvalds."

"I wish you would."

"As a favor to you, I am happy to do it," said the Wizard. Then he said, "Bon Voyage!" gave a half-bow, and, in the way of Wizards, disappeared in a puff of smoke.

• • •

He appeared, quietly, with no smoke or fanfare, in the shadows of a warehouse building along the river Swift. That had gone surprisingly well, thought Dimsbury. It would have pained him to have killed his old schoolmate Weeveston. Not much, but it is worth something to avoid even a momentary pang. To attack the city without resistance would mean his magnificent Orcs would not have their numbers greatly reduced by tonight's Adventure. That pleased Dimsbury and, for a moment, he thought of conquering a bit more of the world.

Ah, but ambition would wait until he had isolated the very source of Magic. And this attack would grant him the peace and quiet he needed. One good long push at the end, and he felt confident he would have it within his grasp. Everything, really. For who could resist a man with limitless power?

But tonight. A respite from his labors. His feet carried him south. He knew of a place–not the finest establishment, or even reputable by the standards of a privileged Mercian upbringing, it is true–but as he had been living on things grown in a cave, it would do.

Yes, a fine roast leg of lamb. Then a pleasant walk to a hilltop from which to watch the city burn. The only thing he regretted was that he would not have good company to enjoy such a delightful evening with. The sacrifices he made for his work were many.

5

Boltac dragged the unconscious Farm Boy out of his shop. He looked around for a place to ditch the kid. Across the street, he saw an empty bench in front of The Bent Eelpout Tavern. Perfect, thought Boltac. He'll be just another drunk on a bench, sleeping it off.

As he dragged the lad across the street, Boltac muttered to himself, "What were you thinking? Loan you a sword? Are you crazy? Well, of course you're crazy. Forget I asked." With much grunting, Boltac propped the lad up on the bench. He looked up at the hideous, twisted fish on the Tavern's faded sign and a longing for ale filled him.

"Look kid," he said to the gently snoring Farm Boy on the bench, "It's for your own good. I mean, if you didn't see that coming, you're not going to see anything else coming. And that wasn't even tricky. You know what's tricky? Adventures are tricky." Boltac sighed heavily. "Believe me, go back to the farm."

Boltac watched the sleeping boy for a moment. Unconscious he seemed even younger. "Okay, no charge for the concussion. And you're welcome," Boltac said. Then he went inside.

"Asarah, my love!" Boltac bellowed before the door had even had a chance to close behind him, "I have come to rescue you from all of this."

The harried, hard-working, beautiful mistress of the inn turned away from the table she was clearing. She flung a lock of dark hair out of her face and saw that it was Boltac. Her professional smile fell from her face and she asked, "And who's going to rescue you?"

Boltac climbed up on a bar stool and said, "No, no. I mean it this time. I have come to sweep you away from all this pointless drudgery. We shall journey to a far Kingdom where I am Lord and Master, and you will be my Queen."

Asarah walked behind the bar and set her hands on the well-worn wooden top. "Whattaya want, Boltac?"

Eying the beautiful, dark-haired woman before him, Boltac had the courage to tell the truth because it would play as a joke. "Only you, my love."

"Yeah, well, all you've got is money, Boltac. And I ain't for sale. Now what are you having?"

"Asarah, can I borrow an ale?"

"What? Borrow an ale?"

"My point exactly!"

"Borrow?"

"Yes."

"Who asks such a thing?"

"Precisely!" said Boltac, pounding his fist on the bar. "Who asks such a thing? But people do. I swear to the Gods they do. A young man, not 20 minutes ago, walked into my store and had the nerve to ask me if he could borrow a sword."

"What? You mean like you'd ask a neighbor to borrow a cup of sugar?"

"Yes, exactly. Except when you borrow a cup of sugar, you don't go off and use it to get yourself killed trying to save some damn fool Priestess of Dar."

"Oh, virgin love," she said as a moony look crept into her eye.

"En-henh," said Boltac. "How about I just rent an ale?"

"Comin' right up." Asarah drew a tankard of ale from the keg and set it on the bar in front of Boltac. Then she asked, "So, did you loan him the sword?"

"No," snapped Boltac, foam flying from his lips as his blissful first sip was interrupted by the memory of the recent inanity. "I hit him over the head with a club, dragged him across the street, and left him unconscious on the bench out front."

Asarah's eyes grew dark with anger. "How *could* you?"

"It was easy, actually, I just took my... Look, woman, when you pick up a sword you pick up a lot of other things with it. And if the lad wasn't ready to deal with the ambush of a shopkeeper with a trick knee, then he certainly wasn't ready to deal with whatever dangerous and vile thing he meant to bash in the head of to preserve the Honor of his wench."

"That word again. Wench. I thought you said she was a Priestess."

"Oh, come on, it was a Sleeping Beauty. They were roping him."

"You don't know that. It could have been True Love. True romantic Love. The kind that you only hear about in songs."

"Yeah, you only hear about it in the songs, because ain't real."

"Your heart is full of money," said Asarah. "Money and mistrust."

"No," said Boltac, "It's not full. There's room for more money." Asarah rolled her eyes. "Besides, that's not the point. It's not about my heart. My head is filled with common sense. Say he's not being conned–which is unlikely, but what the hell–so I give him the sword, and he goes and gets himself killed. Then that's on me, and for what?"

"But that's how she will know. The only way she can know!"

"Know what, he's an idiot?"

"The girl, she's in danger right?"

"I think it was something more along the lines of a fight for her Honor, but sure, let's say she's in danger."

"Danger. She's been kidnapped, let's say. And she's being held captive at the bottom of horrible dungeon."

"Certainly are plenty of horrible dungeons around Robrecht," said Boltac, looking around the room for another subject.

"It's so romantic. And he goes to rescue her and when he *does* rescue her that's how she *knows*."

"Eeeeyeah. You keep saying that. Knows what?"

"That he *Loves* her. When he risks everything he has, when she sees that he's willing to give it all up, that's how she will know he really, truly Loves her above all others."

"That's how she'll know he's a muscle-headed idiot who's good with a sword."

"But he can't because some fat, greedy Merchant wouldn't loan him a sword."

"No," said Boltac, struggling with his anger, "I could loan him a sword and armor and everything else in my store, and it wouldn't make a difference. He can't because he DOESN'T KNOW HOW TO USE A SWORD!"

"Keep your voice down," hissed Asarah. "You're disturbing the other patrons!"

"Patron," quipped Boltac as he gestured toward the nearly empty common room with his empty tankard.

Asarah slammed another ale down in front of him and said. "There's no romance in your life. No passion. No wonder you are alone. I feel sorry for you Boltac." And then she stormed off into the back.

"Safer that way," Boltac muttered into his beer.

Behind Boltac, the door opened and an unseasonably cool wind filled the inn. A man in a black robe with a silver torque around his neck seemed to float across the common room as the door shut behind him. He took in the room with a raised eyebrow of disapproval then made his way to the bar. He sat and asked Boltac, "Do they have lamb tonight?"

"They usually do."

"Hmm, good. Good."

"So stranger, what business brings you to our fair city?" asked Boltac.

"Hmm, city?" asked the man, with a shake of his head, "Ashtantis, that's a city. Squalipoor, Yorn, those are cities. This is a fish-drying village with delusions of grandeur."

"More like delusions of Glory," said Boltac as he raised his ale, not sure he liked the other man's tone. "You have traveled then, a trader?" asked Boltac, sniffing around for a profit.

"More of a wandering scholar," said the man.

"What have you learned here?" Boltac asked, sure that the man wasn't a scholar, but playing along anyway.

"I have learned that this dismal little inn serves the finest leg of lamb I have ever had."

On cue, Asarah emerged from the kitchen and gave Boltac a withering glare.

"You should tell her that," Boltac said. Asarah noticed the new customer at the bar and replaced her frown with a smile.

"Madame, I have traveled many miles today, and all of them were in anticipation of the meal I hope to have at your establishment. Please, tell me you have made your incomparable lamb this evening."

Asarah's smile widened into one of true pleasure. She blushed and curtsied. "Well, I don't know about incomparable, but we do have roasted lamb tonight."

"A leg if you please," said the man in black robes, "and an ale."

"Of course, it's a pleasure to serve such a refined customer," Asarah said, and smiled at him in a way that Boltac didn't like. Asarah slid the man his ale and hurried back to the kitchen.

Boltac called after her. "Make that two." Without looking back Asarah threw him a dismissive wave over her shoulder.

For a moment, both men sat quietly with their ales. The man in black robes staring into space thoughtfully. Boltac staring at the door through which Asarah had just disappeared. The stranger broke the silence first. "What is an Eelpout?"

"An Eelpout? You don't know what an Eelpout is?"

"I am, as they say, not from around here."

"Eeh, yeah, no doubt. So an Eelpout is, well, imagine an ugly fish."

The Man in Black's expression did not change.

"Seriously, envision it in your head."

"I am."

"Oh, well, then it's nowhere near ugly enough. It's so ugly, this Eelpout, that to think of it is to–"

"I have seen a great many ugly things," said the man in a way that indicated that he, the far worldlier man, was growing tired of this exchange.

"But you've never seen an Eelpout, is what I'm saying."

"No."

"Ugliest Godsdamned fish in the world."

"And bent?"

"Drunk, I'd guess. Probably nothing uglier in the universe than an Eelpout on a bender."

"Then why would one name an establishment after such a creature?"

"No idea," said Boltac. "Mystery of it all."

"Ah, mystery."

Asarah left the kitchen with a well-laden tray. She threw another high-powered smile at the stranger as she slid a steaming trencher of lamb in front of him. "Your dinner, sir." When she turned to face Boltac, the smile slipped from her face. She slapped the plate in front of him, and delicious, savory lamb juice splattered the front of Boltac's tunic. She turned and walked away without saying a word.

The stranger swallowed his first bite and sighed with true contentment. "The only true mystery is why someone doesn't take such a talented creature away from all this."

Boltac's eyebrows lifted and only his mouth moved as he asked, "In the gentle words of the virgin Priestesses of Dar, come again?"

"Oh, nothing. It's just, such a rare creature. Such a rare talent. I wonder why she stays in this... squalor."

"Squalor? Buddy, I'm eatin' here."

"Oh, I meant no offense. It is what you are *used* to after all."

"En henh. Well, her husband owned this inn. He died, and that's her hand of cards."

"Hmm," the stranger grunted, as he tucked into his dinner in earnest.

"So, uh, while we're asking questions, what's with the dismal garb, friend? If you are in the market for some more impressive garments, I have a fine store but a few steps away."

"Ah, yes. A Merchant. You would be. And as for the dismal garb, I prefer the term humble. I am a, uh, wandering scholar, in search of knowledge."

"Knowledge? Here's something you can always count on: Don't take any wooden nickels," Boltac said, trying to lighten the mood.

"What's a nickel?"

"You don't know what a nickel is? Not much of a scholar, are you?"

"I'm not concerned with insignificant matters like trade and commerce."

"Enh, but still. You know, clothes make the man."

"Ability makes the man."

"Yeah, that too. But nice clothes don't hurt, I'm just saying. My name is Boltac, by the way."

"Dimsbury," the man said, in a way that irritated Boltac. A way that implied a title lurking somewhere in the wings. Who was he to put on airs? Here they were, both in The Bent Eelpout, one as good as the other. If he was so high and mighty why wasn't he gnawing on mutton at the Duke's table? "Forgive me if I don't shake hands," Dimsbury concluded, sealing Boltac's judgment of him.

Dimsbury finished the last bite of lamb and threw a gold piece (more than ten times enough for the bill) on the bar. He said, "See that she gets that, my good man. And ask her to bring me another ale over by the fire. Nothing personal," he said, with a thin-lipped smile, "I have a chill."

As he watched Dimsbury go, Boltac thought, you brought that chill with you, ya rich prick. Then he muttered a prayer to Dallios, "Just get me a chance to negotiate with that guy. He won't feel so high and mighty after that, I promise you." Since there wasn't an offer attached, Dallios didn't hear Boltac's plea. But other, older Gods–the ones in charge of punishing Hubris–they heard Boltac loud and clear.

When Asarah returned and saw the coin on the bar she exclaimed, "What a fine gentleman he turned out to be!" She held up the gold piece and marveled at it.

"Oh yeah. Real prince of a guy. He said that's to cover mine, too. And he wants another ale over by the fire."

Asarah stabbed him with a look. "So nice to have a quality customer for a change."

Boltac held her gaze without flinching. "I'll get outta your hair."

6

Boltac slammed the door of the inn behind him. He was angry at Asarah for reasons he didn't fully comprehend. He looked up at the stars. He looked down at the muddy cobbles at his feet. Then he looked across the square to his store. For a time, he stood in the middle of the square, trapped between inn and store. He paced in a circle, not knowing which way to go. But he avoided looking at the bench where the Farm Boy slept.

Damn what that woman thought! Her fool ideas of Romance and Heroism. Damn the world, for that matter. The boy was an idiot and searching for death. No good to anyone and a great deal of trouble to whomever he meant to poke with whatever sword he could beg, borrow, or steal. That was the thing that all the would-be Heroes forgot. The people they meant to stab to death in the name of Glory thought that they were Heroes too.

In the end, observed Boltac, it wasn't even the Heroes that got the worst of it. It was the people in the middle. The shopkeepers, the peasants, the simple folk just trying to get through the day. To make a buck, raise a crop, or raise a family.

This dark line of thinking steeled Boltac's nerve so he could get across the square. But, when the shop door closed behind him, his resolve faltered. He peered through the window at the boy he had knocked unconscious. For a moment, Boltac was worried that he had killed the lad. But then the boy stirred a little in his sleep.

Boltac remembered when he had been the Farm Boy's age. Young and strong and chained to a store. His father had been fond of saying, "Keep a shop, and it will keep you." And so it did, keeping a young boy from doing anything that he might want to do in this world. Keeping him at endless, boring work that served as torture for a young man who craved Adventure.

He did not feel guilty for braining the lad. If it was Adventure the boy was after, he would have to withstand far worse. And if his younger self had appeared by Magic before him in his own store Boltac would have done far, far worse. He would have worn his arm out trying to beat some sense into his former self.

Why couldn't Asarah see the logic of that? Why did she never approve of Boltac's carefully negotiated ways? He craved her affection and approval more than he understood. But it was a thing of which he could not speak. Even to himself.

There was no way to tell a young man of the hazards that awaited him–of the costs to life and limb and family–of all the ways of hurt and all the ways those hurts could radiate beyond himself. It was a terrible thing to be a Hero. And Boltac wished the pain of it on no one. And on no one's family.

But there was no way to frame the words, no order to put them in that could make it through a testosterone-addled brain and overcome the lust for Glory. If not this Priestess con, the lad would find some other cause, or scrape, or trouble. At least he wasn't off in search of the Evil Wizard all of the other Adventurers were always harassing. None of them ever seemed to come back. Who knew, maybe that meant the Wizard was real and terrible after all.

No, Boltac realized, there was no stopping him. So why had he tried? Because he saw himself in the lad. Because he would have given much to take back the poor choices of his own youth. He spit and cursed the bards. It was all their fault. Putting all these ideas in young men's heads. Sending them off to war or in search of gold.

Damn it all. He stomped to the sword barrel, drew a blade, and tested its balance. Awful. He sighted the edge. It was as curved as an old whore's back. What an awful piece of workmanship. It was the kind of item he would willingly sell to a fool, but not the kind of weapon he would wish on his worst enemy. A man needed a sword he could trust. Boltac saw the shape of a terrible memory rising from the dark waters of his mind. Before the thought could fully take hold, he slammed the sword back in the barrel.

He walked to the rack of weapons. He removed the blade on the bottom. It was the one he would have chosen, if he were spending his own money. It was a stout Mercian sword. At one end, its straight blade came to a broad triangular point. At the other, the hilt was a heavy round pommel that, in the hands of someone who knew what he was doing, qualified as a weapon on its own. The blade sang softly as he unsheathed it and begged to dance in his hand. He sighted this weapon and its hard edge was as crisp, final, and unforgiving as the border between life and death.

There wasn't a soul on the streets as Boltac crossed the square. The stars seemed impossibly high and uncaring. When he got to the Farm Boy, he hung the sword around the lad's neck very carefully, so as not to wake him. Underneath the thick head of straw-blond hair, Boltac could see a freshly-risen lump. Ouch. He reached out to touch it. His fingers almost made contact. Then Boltac became self-conscious. He looked around as if he were afraid of being caught doing something wrong. But there was no one watching. He scuttled back across the square.

7

Back in his shop, Boltac barred the door and retrieved the heavy lockbox from beneath the counter. It hadn't been a busy day, but in dribs and drabs the coins had piled up. He had sold a bit of lace here, a poultice there. It added up to a living.

He poured the coins out on the counter. Then looked out the window and across the square. The boy was there and still unconscious. For an instant, Boltac thought about retrieving the blade. If the kid didn't wake up, surely someone would come along and steal it. But, if Asarah came out and saw the kid with the sword, it would go halfway to getting Boltac back in her good graces. On the other hand, if she came out and caught Boltac taking the sword back... ergh, she'd never forgive him for that. Anyway, she was probably too busy fawning over that slumming aristocrat to tear herself away. That fop, throwing a gold coin away like it was nothing. Who did he think he was? Coins were for being careful with. For counting, for hoarding, for saving for a rainy day.

Boltac divided the coins for the day's sales into three piles on his counter; gold, silver, and copper. He quickly counted the copper coins and made a note of them in his ledger. With the silver coins, he took more time. He used a set of weights and measures to make sure that not only the count was accurate, but also the total weight.

Boltac was very careful not to take any coins that had been clipped, or were too light to be pure. With copper, clipping was rarely a problem. The coins just weren't worth enough to go to the trouble. With silver, clipping became a problem, but that was easily spotted . The gold coins presented the greatest difficulty for Boltac.

Gold coins were worth enough that instead of merely clipping them, counterfeiters would dip lead slugs into molten gold to create a coin that was worth less than silver. This presented a conundrum for a shrewd Merchant who did not want to be taken advantage of. It was insulting to test a customer's coin on the spot, yet painful to take a loss.

Boltac grabbed a small glass dish and a bottle labeled Aqua Fortis from a shelf beneath the counter. He carefully poured the liquid from the bottle into the dish. Then he picked up one of the gold coins, dipped it in the liquid, and examined it carefully. If it had turned green, it would have been a sign that the coin was some alloy, or plated lead. But this coin remained its reassuring yellow color. With a satisfied grunt, he placed the sound coin on the other side of the dish.

He tested coin after coin, pleased to find that all of them were real. Finally, only two coins remained. When he dipped the second-to-last coin of the day, it did not turn green. It did not smoke. It did not sizzle or emit a smell like rotten onions. Instead, it hissed, came to life, and bit his hand.

Boltac cursed and threw the evil little thing across the room. Then he immediately regretted it. With surprising speed for a fat man, he scrambled out from behind the counter and pursued it. In the middle of the floor, the gold coin sprouted thin, insect-like legs and scrabbled for purchase against the boards. Boltac tried to stomp it and missed. He stomped again and again, hopping through his store, knocking items over in a strange, destructive dance. The coin scrambled under a rack of rope and strips of leather. With a roar, Boltac kicked the rack over and brought his booted foot down squarely upon the creature.

"HA!" he cried in triumph. He shambled to the other side of the room, dragging his foot as he went, grinding the creature across the floor, until he was able to reach a set of pliers hanging on the wall. Then he bent down and, ever so carefully, clamped the edge of the angry, savage coin in the teeth of the pliers. It let out another metallic shriek, but Boltac was unmoved by its pain.

He carried the coin into the back, past the foul-smelling bundle of gear he had purchased from Rattick and to a set of iron-bound chests that were sealed with fearsome-looking locks and bolted to the floor. The one on the right had a hole in the top of it, sealed with a piece of cork. He removed the cork, crammed the coin into the hole–having to hit it several times with a hammer to convince it to go in–and then replaced the cork. He put his ear to the chest and listened to the evil thing clawing in vain against the wood. Only when he heard the "clink" of the coin-creature settling down, did he lift his ear from the chest.

Boltac looked to his hand. A fingernail-sized disc of flesh was missing from his palm and blood leaked down his forearm. Damned coin. He kicked the chest and immediately regretted it. The chest didn't move, and all he got for his trouble was a hurt foot. A bad trade.

Boltac smiled and pulled the thong from around his neck. There, amid the countless tokens and charms was a small silver whistle. He grabbed it with his uninjured hand and blew on it for all he was worth. Such a furious, shrieking commotion erupted from inside the chest that Boltac worried it might burst. He imagined the hundreds, maybe thousands, of coins in the cramped, dark space–all angry, all clawing at each other in fury. He smiled.

Boltac had named these treacherous pieces of currency the Creeping Coins. At one time, he had thought to train them to perform, as he had seen traveling mummers train fleas, snakes, monkeys, and even bears. But they were either untrainable or Boltac hadn't the knack for it. For all his time and experimentation, he had earned only some nasty bite scars and the knowledge that a certain high-pitched frequency drove the Creeping Coins mad.

Who had created these creatures, and why? Boltac had been unable to find out. What he had learned was that they were a species of Magical animal that preferred to stay unseen. They had a most sinister method of reproduction. If you placed one of these Magic

52

coins in a pile of regular coins, they would slowly but surely convert all of the real money to animated hunks of metal with sharp little teeth. One at a time, they were an annoyance. But in the depths of a dungeon, in a chest full of gold that might not be opened for years? These creatures could turn a payday into a nightmare.

He rubbed a healing ointment into the fingernail-sized bite in his hand. It stopped the bleeding but did nothing for the pain. What could a school of these things do? Or just a few of them under a suit of armor? He shuddered. At least death by Dragon would be quicker.

But that's the way it was with any enterprise. People feared the big things, but it was always the little things that did you in. The demons were in the details, as they said. All the work you spent polishing your shield in preparation for a basilisk would be lost if you forgot to bring oil to protect it from rust.

It was a terrible business, Adventuring. Another reason Boltac was glad he had grown up, settled down, and learned to enjoy a warm fire and a crisp profit. Again, he reassured himself that he had done that lad a favor by knocking him on the head.

8

As Dimsbury sat with his feet by the fire, it took him a good hour to give a name to what he was feeling. Contentment didn't quite do it. Comfort was part of it, but there was something else. A warmish feeling in the stomach that he was quite unaccustomed to. There was something about a good meal after a good day's work. His plans all in order, everything tilting and tending the way it should. Sated, yes, that was the word he was looking for. He felt sated.

For a moment, he considered ordering another whole dinner. But there was no time. He had completed his errand and should really leave the city before the carnage started. But perhaps he should take a leg of mutton to go. Or—would they have such a thing—some mutton sandwiches?

It was so hard to get good food at the bottom of a dungeon. Yes, he had servants, but they were creations. Not flesh and blood. They viewed roasting as an information-gathering technique, or at best a method of discipline, not as an essential part of cuisine. And spices? Well, Orcs are rare minerals and raw flesh. It was a practice guaranteed to keep the palate in an unrefined state.

None of this even touched on the degradation of his decor and living conditions. Of course, the Wizard could have taken some pains on his own behalf, but there was his work to think of. All else paled in comparison to that. But even here, in this homey inn, the Wizard felt a longing for the comfort he had almost forgotten he could have. A woman's touch. Yes, that was the phrase.

When the wench came around again, he asked, "Do you make sandwiches? You know, to go?"

"My sandwiches are so good, men have proposed to me after the first bite," said Asarah with a playful toss of her hair.

Outside, a wolf howled.

"What was that?" Asarah asked, her smile becoming tainted with concern.

She had a nice smile, and the Wizard thought it was all the sweeter for being mixed with fear. Oh yes, thought the Wizard, he would definitely be taking something to go. "It sounded like a wolf," he said with exaggerated innocence. "I'd like two mutton sandwiches, please." He smiled.

"With lettuce and tomato?" asked Asarah.

"However you like them."

"Well, you could enjoy the hospitality of The Bent Eelpout and take fresh ones with you in the morning. Evidently, there are wolves about."

The Wizard smiled again. "But what assurance do I have that it will still be here in the morning?"

"What, the sandwich?"

"No. The inn."

9

When Boltac heard the howl, he looked up and out the front window. Across the square, the boy still slept in the moonlight. Boltac stood motionless, watching, with the last gold coin clamped in his pliers. After having been bitten, he was taking no more chances. All coins were now guilty until proven innocent.

The peaceful scene outside his window did not change, so Boltac shrugged and touched the coin to the acid. It did not come to life and attack him, so he dropped it in the pile with the others.

He carefully poured the acid back into the bottle and wiped down the counter. Then he gathered up the coins and carried them into the back. He placed them in the other chest, the one that held the normal coins. Then he turned his attention to the pile of soiled goods he had purchased from Rattick.

From the corner of his eye, he caught a flash of something moving past the window. He looked up and out the front of the store. There was a flash of grey. And then again.

Boltac walked forward slowly. He had no idea what was going on, but he was pretty sure he didn't like it. It was out of the ordinary. And, in Boltac's experience, anything out of the ordinary was bad for business. In the distance, he heard someone sound a horn. Then, he thought he could hear a woman scream. Or maybe it was a horse? What was going on?

He stepped outside into the empty square. To the north, across the river, he saw the red glow of fire. Ah, thought Boltac: Raiders. He knew this game all too well. He had hoped that the new Duke's garrison was strong enough to keep the Raiders out. The tariffs and taxes from a crossroads town like Robrecht were valuable. As long as Boltac had been here, the nobles and empires of the world had passed Robrecht back and forth like a toy.

They didn't even pretend to install a King anymore. Robrecht had been pillaged so many times it didn't even get to keep the illusion of being its own state. It had been reduced to a mere protectorate. "En henh," Boltac grumbled. There was scant protection to be found in a protectorate.

Maybe if the Duke had released his tax collectors on the invaders? That might have done it. Boltac shook his head and went inside. He pulled his stool out from behind the counter and set to loading crossbows. Just let them come, thought Boltac grimly; they would find his prices very, very high indeed.

Across the square, he watched the Man in Black emerge from the Tavern holding two sandwiches wrapped in parchment.

"Heh," said Boltac, "if they come across the river, this prick sure is in for a surprise."

The Man in Black took notice of the Farm Boy, still asleep on the bench. He looked him up and down. Then he nudged the lad with his toe.

"Some Adventurer," muttered Boltac, "he doesn't even wake up! Did I ever do that kid a favor."

The Man in Black reached into his pocket and produced a whistle. He put it to his lips and blew it. It produced a slightly lower note than the whistle Boltac had used on the coins. The Man in Black sounded the note three times, and then waited.

Boltac heard them coming before he saw them. It sounded like a crowd saying something like, "Hork, Hork, Hork, Hork!" From the darkness came the largest wolves Boltac had ever seen. As they advanced, they snarled and snapped at each other and their riders.

Whistles, thought Boltac, I knew it had to be done with whistles!

Boltac shrank back from the window as one of the wolves sniffed at it and fogged the glass. What in the Gods' name were they? And the men that rode on their backs? They seemed more animal than man. Their greyish green skin looked thick and inhuman, as if it should have scales. Their evil little eyes were set too close together. Their proportionally small mouths were overflowing with teeth, and gave the impression they would gnaw rather than chew. They had large, wide noses and pointed ears set high on their heads.

"Ah," thought Boltac, "These would be Orcs."

There was no way Rattick had fought one of those things. And there was no way they wore jewelry. Perhaps a necklace made of ears, but not expensive rubies.

The Orcs converged on the Man in Black. For a moment, Boltac thought the wolves would tear the man's face off. But then the Man in Black said something and the growls and snarls changed to frightened whimpers. Two of the Orcs dismounted and their wolves ran away.

The Orcs turned as if to chase after their steeds, but a sharp bark from the Man in Black stopped them. Who was this man who commanded monsters, Boltac wondered?

Boltac sighted his crossbow on the Man in Black, and then thought better of it. After all, he wasn't involved in this transaction. He should stay calm, keep his head down, and hope they passed his store by. That was the surest way to avoid a loss in this situation. At least that's what his head told him. But his heart offered a different commentary as he watched the two Orcs kick in the door of The Bent Eelpout.

Asarah!

She'd be fine, Boltac told himself. She was a strong woman and used to dealing with unruly customers. She had come through raids before. She'd be fine. The Man in Black dismissed the remaining, still-mounted Orcs. The... whattaya call a bunch of Orcs anyway? A troupe, a band, a herd, a gaggle? Anyway, the rest of them rode south.

With a crossbow in the crook of his right arm, not taking his eyes from the square, he eased back to the weapons rack and grabbed a double-headed axe without looking at it.

He asked himself, "What are you doing? Asking for trouble, that's what. Don't do anything stupid. You're a Merchant, not a Hero. She'll be fine. You're no help to anybody dead." Then he placed the axe, head down, beneath the windowsill, beside the other crossbow.

Across the square, he saw the two Orcs emerge from the inn holding Asarah between them. She struggled against them and cursed.

"Still think she is going to be okay?" he asked the voice in his head. It didn't answer.

The Man in Black turned to look at Asarah, and she spit on him. Then the Man in Black struck her across the face. Knocked sideways from the blow, Asarah struggled to bring her head upright again and roll her hair out of her eyes. The Man in Black stood with his back to Boltac's store, so that Boltac could not see his face. Whatever expression the unpleasant man wore, when Asarah saw it she screamed.

Something broke inside of Boltac. Before he knew what he was doing, he had fired both crossbows and was charging out the door with the axe in hand. The first crossbow bolt took the Orc on Asarah's left in the throat. The second hit the other Orc in the shoulder.

Asarah screamed a plea and a question, "Boltac?"

But the Boltac she knew was no longer there. The rational, calcu-lating, cunning Merchant who stuck his neck out for nobody was not the same creature whose lungs burned and heart pumped as his feet pounded across the cobblestones. *That* Boltac was lifting the axe and imagining cleaving the Man in Black from neck to breastbone.

That Boltac didn't hear it coming until it was too late.

If it had been a man on a horse riding him down, he would have heard him coming from a week away. But the pads of a wolf on the cobblestones? He realized his mistake when it was too late. The wolf's fangs sank into his shoulder and lifted him from the ground at a dead run.

"HORRRRRRRRRRRRRRK!" cried the triumphant Orc.

In pain and with animal rage, Boltac slashed blindly with the axe. He felt the edge sink deep into the wolf's neck. He heard it grunt in pain. The pressure in his shoulder went away as the wolf let go. Wolf, Orc, and shopkeeper tumbled across the cobblestones and landed in a heap. Somehow, Boltac kept his grip on the axe.

In a haze, he watched Asarah struggling with the Man in Black. She was shouting, but the only thing Boltac could hear was the pounding of his own heart. He pulled himself from beneath the wolf, tried to stand, and failed. His knee folded sideways underneath him. The pain from the second fall was worse than the first. Clutching the axe, he started to crawl.

Behind him, the Orc got to his feet and recovered his pike. He cocked his head sideways at this strange man crawling towards The Master. Then he lifted his weapon and went to finish him.

"Hold!" commanded the Man in Black. The Orc stayed the final blow.

"My, my, my, but you *are* determined," said the Man in Black with an air of amusement that made Boltac hate him even more. "You are something more than a Merchant, I think," said the Wizard.

"En-henh," Boltac said, and kept crawling.

"Boltac, what are you doing?" asked Asarah. Boltac could not answer because he was fighting off a wave of pain. But still he crawled. He was oblivious to the pike above his head and only aware of the Man in Black's expensive boots in front of him. He was going to cut the bastard's feet off and see where it went from there.

Dimsbury shook his head at the poor spectacle beneath him. A fat

Merchant, crawling to his death as the hot stuff of life trailed on the cobbles behind him. How was it that the poor Merchant's arm had not been completely severed? He turned to his prize. "Come, my dear, let me take you away from all of this."

"Let me go!" she cried, "I must tend my inn."

"Ah, yes," said Dimsbury. He waved his hand without taking his eyes from her, and the front of The Bent Eelpout was engulfed in flame.

Asarah screamed again.

"Please," said Dimsbury, "refrain from screaming in my ear." To the Orc he said, "Finish him." Then he gripped Asarah around the waist and held her to him. Before she could struggle, he took flight and disappeared straight up into the night with her.

Boltac fought his way to his knees and reached after her.

The Orc brought the butt end of his pike down on Boltac's back and knocked him to the ground. Boltac heard some of his ribs separate from his spine. He thought that was bad, until the Orc kicked him in those same ribs. His world went white with pain and Boltac rolled over onto his back.

This was it. The Orc spun the pike and touched him gently on the nose with the point. Then lifted the pike into the air for the coup de grace.

In that final moment, Boltac discovered that he wasn't afraid. He wasn't even angry. His last thought was of Asarah, and he was sad. Sad that he would never get to see her again. Sad that he would never again get to play the game of cheating her out of a drink, or drive her mad with his haggling, or marvel at the way her hair would bounce and turn like a living thing as she worked her way through the common room of her inn.

At times like these, ordinary men try negotiating with death. They offer every promise, pledge, and advantage they can think of in exchange for life. But Boltac was not an ordinary man. And certainly not an ordinary negotiator. At that moment, he realized that his life alone was not worth negotiating for. If he was to haggle with fate, it would not be for his life–it would not be for his store or his fortune. Boltac was surprised to discover that, in the final accounting, those things were worth nothing to him. The only thing worth negotiating for was life with *her*. Without her, he couldn't come up with a reason to bother.

As if in a dream, he watched two feet of steel blade emerge from the Orc's belly. The pike fell, not on Boltac's head, but next to him on the cobbled street. As the Orc's body fell away to one side, Boltac saw the Farm Boy standing there, trying to hold the Orc up with the sword Boltac had given him. No scream of victory echoed from the boy's throat. Instead, he looked at the blood and the blade and the corpse that was dragging his hand towards the ground as if he couldn't quite understand what had just happened.

"That blade is a quality item," Boltac said. Then he passed out.

10

The Farm Boy was so terrified he left the sword in the Orc.

"Mister? Mister? What do I do?"

"Henh?" said Boltac, wondering why he wasn't being left to die in peace. Then he realized that he wasn't dead, but was in a tremendous amount of pain. "The store, get me to the store."

"Okay, I can do that."

"Good kid. I'm gonna pass out now." But as soon as the mule-strong Farm Boy started dragging him across the cobbles, the pain of his injuries brought him back to consciousness. "Ahhhhh–AHHHH!"

"Sorry," said the Farm Boy.

"Don't apologize. Just draAAAAAAAAAHag!" Boltac screamed, then passed out from the pain.

When the Farm Boy got Boltac into the store, he propped him up against the counter. Boltac came around enough to say, "Take the keys. In the back, the chest on the left. Very important, only open the chest on the LEFT. Bring me the bottle."

"Which bottle?"

"The *only* bottle. And hurry up. I'm dyin' here!"

"The only bottle. Right."

The Farm Boy hurried to the back. Fear caused him to fumble with the lock. And drop the keys. He had never seen that much blood come from a person before. And that thing he had stabbed out there. What was that? He hadn't really thought about it. He'd woken up and seen it about to kill the Merchant. There had been a sword in his lap. There had been no time. He had just done what needed doing.

He dropped the keys again. He never thought it would be anything like this. They sure didn't sing about this part. What if more of them came? What if they could smell blood? What if they were coming to the shop right now? Had he shut the door? And if he had shut the door, had he remembered to bar it? He was confused and his head really, really hurt.

He opened the chest. Inside were many leather bags filled with coins. Ye Gods, how many coins were in here? Tucked in a corner was a cut-glass bottle with the stopper wired shut. It seemed very old, and the edges of the bottle were painted with gold leaf. The Farm Boy picked it up very carefully. Drop the keys all you want, he told himself, but don't drop this bottle.

He carried it out to where Boltac sat propped up in a pool of his own blood. As he handed it to Boltac, he heard a buzzing as if an angry hive of bees were close by and with it, the smell of burning wood. "Gods," the Farm Boy exclaimed, "flaming bees!"

"Shut up, kid," Boltac said weakly, knowing that it was only the Magic-detecting wand under the counter reacting to the potency of what was in the bottle. "It's Magic. Now, undo the wire."

The Farm Boy did as he was asked. Boltac held the bottle in his left hand and took the cork out with his teeth. He spit it across the room. Then he raised the bottle in a toast and said, "Listen, kid, if I don't make it. All this..."–he indicated the store he had worked so hard to build–"You don't take a single friggin' thing, you understand? I wanna be buried with *all* of it."

Up until that point, the Farm Boy hadn't thought of stealing. It wasn't what Heroes did, so it wasn't what the Farm Boy would do. But now he couldn't help himself. As Boltac drank the bottle, the lad looked around. But when Boltac screamed in pain, the Farm Boy's attention snapped back to the shopkeeper.

Boltac writhed and his back arched at a frightful angle. There was a snapping and popping noise as his knee twisted back into place on its own. Sweat poured from Boltac's face as he spiked a fever and broke it in less than a minute. A wave of nausea came, and then a sense of calm. The ragged wound in his shoulder spit out a wickedly curved tooth and closed.

"Wh-wh-wh-what was that?" the Farm Boy asked in amazement.

"That," Boltac said, the snap returning to his voice, "was a *Magic* potion. The genuine article. Most of what I sell is herbs and healing tonics, a couple of smelly poultices made by this old crone out in one of the villages. I won't say they're garbage, but uh, you slap a poultice on a serious wound? Ya gonna die."

"Do you have any more?" the Farm Boy asked with wide eyes. Carrying a few of those potions with him would be an antidote to the fear that was still causing his limbs to shake.

"Ah, no. Very rare. Very expensive. Help me up."

Boltac tried his recently mangled leg. It felt good. In fact, it felt better than he could remember it ever feeling.

"Are you okay?" asked the Farm Boy.

"En-henh."

"What are you going to do?"

"What am I going to do?" Boltac thought hard. Set his jaw, narrowed his eyes and then fell dead asleep on his feet. He didn't even wake up when he hit the floor.

11

When Boltac awoke, he found himself in his bed. Bright light streamed in through the window and he was, inexplicably, alive. He returned to consciousness slowly and from a great distance. At first he couldn't remember how he had gotten here, or what had happened. Then, as the memory of it flooded back, he became fearful. Unable, at first, to separate fantastic dream from terrible reality, he flung back the covers. His leg was straight. His shirt was ripped, but the skin underneath was perfect and unscarred. That really had been a *Magic* potion. Hell of a way to find out.

He got out of bed and stretched. Then he went downstairs.

At the foot of the narrow stairs, he found the Farm Boy asleep in a pile of cloaks. Even in his sleep he clutched the sword Boltac had given him. When Boltac nudged him with his boot, the lad awoke with a start.

"Ahh!" screamed the Farm Boy, jumping back. When he saw it was Boltac he said, "I was standing guard. In case those things came back."

"No kid, that's *sleeping* guard." Boltac softened a little. "But, uh, I appreciate it." He stepped over the boy and brought out a loaf of thick black bread and some butter. "C'mon, breakfast."

They ate in silence for a time. Finally, Boltac asked, "Do you have a name?"

"In my village, they call me Relan."

"En-henh," said Boltac. "I thank you, Relan. You saved my life."

Relan asked, "What were those things?"

"Evidently, what you killed was an Orc."

"An Orc?"

"An Orc," Boltac said with a shrug, to indicate that he wasn't the guy making the rules.

"So they were bad," said Relan.

"Yeah, kid, they were definitely bad."

"Are we going to go get them?"

"We? No. I'm not going to go get them. That's why I pay taxes."

"But that Evil Wizard took the woman you Love!"

"Love is a strong word to use, for a pleasant association. Besides, I'm a Merchant, not a fighter."

"If you're not in Love with her, why did you charge out of your store to save her?"

"I, uh... hey, look. It's complicated."

"And if you're not a fighter, how did you manage to kill two Orcs?"

"And a wolf," said Boltac, shaking his head.

"That's pretty good."

"That's only because you suck," snapped Boltac.

"Suck or not, I'm going after that Wizard. Somebody has to do the right thing."

"Kid, the right thing to do is almost always to keep your head down and make a buck."

"That sounds like something a coward would say."

"Eh-henh. It's the kind of thing the living says. Get this, I was very stupid. And I am lucky to be alive. So I am not gonna push my luck. Besides, this kind of thing is why I pay taxes. Let the guards deal with this."

"You're a coward," said Relan.

"Whattaya want from me? I'm a Merchant. I ain't no Hero."

"Well, why would anybody want to be that?" asked Relan. "If the whole world were Merchants, nobody would have saved your life."

"If the whole world was Merchants, everybody would buy and sell instead of stab and hack," snapped Boltac. "Look, I'm grateful for your help. It's not like I'm not grateful. So, uh, as a reward, take what you like from the store–as much as you can carry without horse or wagon–and then go to your death. Have fun. Me, I'm going to find the Duke and see what he's gonna do about all this. See if he can get my innkeeper lady friend back."

Relan shook his head and took another bite of bread.

12

When Boltac stepped outside, he was greeted by smoke hanging thick in the air. Everywhere, there were signs of carnage. The Bent Eelpout and most of the other side of the street had burned to the ground. Boltac saw the dead wolf and Orcs, but did not linger over them.

He turned and headed north. On his walk, he passed several bodies lying in the street. One was a young girl, maybe nine. Her pretty dress was torn and soaked with blood. Boltac looked away from her corpse and muttered, "Bad for business," as if the phrase was a charm that could ward off emotion.

As he crossed the bridge to the keep, he expected to see a line of petitioners. But there was no one. Not even a guard at the gate. The court should have been full of angry citizens demanding redress and protection. The walls should have been decorated with Orcs' heads on pikes. By now, he should have been able to hear wounded members of the Ducal Guard drinking by the stables. Their laughter and the exaggerated stories of their bravery should have carried over the wall. There should have been smoke from the blacksmith, and the sound of weapons being sharpened.

But there was nothing.

In the courtyard, he passed the royal carriage standing all alone. It looked like someone had abandoned it in haste. From the stable, he heard the whinny of a horse.

Boltac pushed his way through the half-opened door and into the keep. There was no one in the antechamber. There was no one anywhere. Every room he checked was empty. It was as if all the people had simply vanished. He cried out, but only the echo of his own hello answered.

When he reached the empty throne room the penny dropped. Mostly, it was the tapestry flapping in a wind that shouldn't have been blowing. Behind the heavy, musty, overly stylized scene of a Heroic battle that had never happened, Boltac found a secret door. Behind the door was a staircase.

He followed it down and down again, through narrow stone passageways until he emerged at a set of docks hidden in a high-walled cove on the north side of the island. From this island in the middle of the river Swift, he could see that all the boats were gone. Discarded items were strewn everywhere. Over there was a guard's helmet; at his feet was a chest of silks. He could almost see the scene as it had happened:

A woman, clamoring, shrieking for her handmaiden or a guard to bring the chest of rich silks onto the boats. But, of course, there is no room for such things. Someone knocking the chest to the docks. Throwing the woman into a boat. Jumping in after her and pushing the craft out into the current.

The water would have taken them south quickly. If they survived the uncomfortable ride through the rapids, they would already be out of the grey, mist-covered mountains of Robrecht and enjoying a leisurely ride to Shatnapur, the northernmost city in the Southron Kingdoms. Odds were they were all free and clear, floating down a river with the sun in their faces.

The guards would know how close they came, but the nobles–the soft and careless ones who claimed privilege to rule–would be thinking only of what Southron delicacies they might feast upon in a few days' time. Rare tropical fruits. The brains of monkeys. Anything delectable and procured at great suffering to the peasantry. What they weren't thinking about, Boltac knew, was the body of a young girl, dead in a gutter.

Boltac spit in the river, then climbed back up the stairs.

Back in the throne room, he tried to wrap his head around it. There was no one. They had *all* gone. At the first sign of danger, the Duke had fled. Boltac walked to the throne and sat down. For a second, he almost took it seriously. Then he laughed at himself.

This wasn't the chair for him. He was a Merchant. Everyone knew you couldn't buy a throne. Of course, such a thing could be inherited. But at some point a throne had to be won, with a sword. A sword drenched in blood. An illiterate barbarian could sooner be a King than a fat Merchant. And it had been so long since Robrecht had had a real King. Or anything other than a figurehead installed by a larger, more powerful Kingdom seeking to control the trade routes.

The health of Kingdoms, thought Boltac, depended not on war but on commerce. The opportunity for everyone to conduct their little businesses in peace was what kept people happy and productive. But, for some reason, the only people deemed fit to rule were warriors and their inbred descendants. Something was wrong with this logic. But it was not for him to fix.

Boltac heaved himself off the fancy chair and left the room. Over the wall of the castle, he saw heavy columns of smoke rising from the north end of town. In twos and threes, people fled from the north gate. To the south, the damage was less but there was a larger stream of traffic. People were leaving. Was this the way it was to be? Was this how his town died?

13

By the time Boltac returned to the store, Relan was gone. Boltac's shopkeeper's eye quickly saw what the boy had taken. All the wrong things. The idiot was probably even walking. Walking to his Heroic death.

Boltac thought about opening for business. He thought about barricading the store against looters. Then he looked across the street to the still-smoldering remnants of The Bent Eelpout. He stared for a long time. He stared until a light rain began to fall. He watched the drops turn to steam as soon as they hit the smoldering coals of what used to be an inn. Each drop was infinitesimal. Wasted. A single drop could not put out a fire. But enough water could wash an entire city away. He savored his melancholy and rolled this thought around for a while. Then he turned his back on the window.

Boltac looked around his store. Not only had the kid had taken all the wrong things, he had taken all the wrong things to carry them in. Boltac shook his head. Why travel if you don't have the luggage you need to enjoy the journey? He had sold a lot of luggage with that line, but that didn't stop it from being good advice.

He went into the back and opened the chest on the left. He took out all of the small leather bags filled with coin and set them aside. He would need money, of course. After all, it was the most multipurpose substance known to man. But, for Boltac's purposes, there was something in here more valuable than money.

"Ah HA!" he said as he held up a burlap sack. The sack looked like its only purpose in life was to hold twenty pounds of potatoes. "There you are," Boltac said to the sack as if to a precious child he had found in a game of hide and seek. Of course, this was a ridiculous analogy–Boltac hated children–but this burlap sack? He couldn't have been more proud of the sack.

He walked through his well-stocked store finding items he might need for a journey to the depths of some foul, unknowable place. Into the sack's modest opening he placed five goatskins of water, two of wine, ten stout torches, a few flagons of the finest oil, three daggers, an axe, an ornate and well-jeweled silver mace in a wooden case, a roll of rare tools used for the picking of locks and dismantling of doors and chests, several hundred feet of good rope, an extra pair of boots, two hats, several wool blankets, a lambswool sweater (the depths could be cold) a side of pork cured in salt, five pounds of hard biscuit, and a pound of chocolate.

But that wasn't all. He flitted here and there among the shelves, adding this, that, and the other—oddments and ointments—anything Boltac thought he might need. Because if Boltac knew one thing about Adventure, it was that you never knew.

The second-to-last thing to go in was the Magic Lantern of Lamptopolis. And very last of all, his thick wool Gauntlets of Magic Negation. Didn't want to be reaching around in a bag like that with bare hands, that's for sure.

Through all of this, the bag never bulged or grew heavier than the 17 or 20 pounds that a sack that size, filled with potatoes, could be expected to weigh. The more Boltac stuffed into the sack, the wider he smiled. For a moment, he considered trying to fit EVERYTHING into the sack, just to see if he could. But then he thought better of it. Even a Magic sack had to have its limits. And if it didn't? That wasn't the kind of thing Boltac wanted to know.

Boltac hated Magic, but he loved this bag. It was Themistres' Bag of Holding. One of only a very few known to exist. It was said that it would contain anything the owner could place into it. It never got heavier or bigger. It was, in effect, a bottomless bag.

Themistres, as the story went, made the bag for his wife. She was a large woman who liked to travel heavy. The Wizard had not made many of them, and no Wizard seemed to have been able to duplicate his feat. Wizards seldom married, and the ones who did, generally wound up turning their wives into something that wouldn't bother them. The Bag of Holding was generally believed to be a myth, a pleasant fiction of overloaded husbands and servants everywhere. But Boltac had found one. And what a wondrous thing it was. Priceless, really.

With this thought of pricing, he remembered the coins he left out in the back. He took out his mittens and put them on. He removed the Magic Lantern from the sack. It did not light as he touched it. Then, he added some gold to the sack. As he did, Boltac wondered: what was the point of holding any in reserve? It wasn't like he expected to be coming back. And that's when Boltac realized–told the truth of it to himself–he probably wasn't going to make it out of this Adventure alive.

He stopped and stood up in the back room of his store. He had worked so hard to build this store into a thriving business. Now, standing among the money he had worked so hard to accumulate, all of it seemed worthless. The heavy weight of the Gauntlets of Magic Negation dragged his hands towards the floor, and his shoulders stooped. For a moment, tears ran down his round, weathered face. He let out one sob. Then sniffed and bent back to the task at hand.

He piled *all* the gold into the sack. Who knew, perhaps he could buy his way out of this trouble? That was what a shrewd Merchant would do.

When he picked up the lamp this time, even though he was still wearing the mittens, a faint light shone out from its depths. Boltac didn't notice.

Boltac left his store and headed north, for points unknown and unknowable. Yes, it was stupid. But there was nothing else to do. In the end, he had no more choice than a single raindrop falling onto the smoldering remains of a burned building. But that didn't mean he didn't have any choices. It had been a mistake to try to fight like a Hero. Boltac could see that now. He wasn't a Hero. He wasn't a King either. But he wasn't powerless. Rather than go off half-cocked, he could use the skills and tools he had. He could do a better job of outfitting himself. And he would be damned if he would be *walking* to his death.

14

Relan was wearing a new pair of boots. In fact, this was his first ever pair of boots of any kind. Up until this point he had worn only sandals or wooden shoes. And those had been hand-me-downs. In one way or another, it seemed that everything in Relan's life had been a hand-me-down. That's the way it was when you were the youngest of seven on a cold-water farm hidden away in the fog-shrouded mountains of Robrecht. There was plenty of work and nothing else.

But if they could see him now?

Over a linen tunic, he wore a shirt of shining chain mail. It wasn't the best mail that Boltac had, but it was the best-looking. Around his neck, a cloak made of hammered felt was clasped with a chain of silver. On his hip, the sword Boltac had given him swung from a wide leather sword belt. On his opposite hip was a dirk with its handle worked into the shape of a screaming eagle. Pants of the finest, softest deer skin he had ever encountered were tucked into the black boots, which had high cuffs and silver buckles. This is how a Hero should look, he thought.

Oh, they had laughed at him on the farm–well, his older brothers and sisters had, Ma and Pa had been too tired. They took the news of his departure as they took all news, good or bad, with the tired stare of someone who has seen the worst that the seasons and the ways of man have had to offer. From long habit, they tried not to get excited one way or the other.

"You'll be back," his eldest brother had said, in imitation of the hard, bitter speech of his father. But then his stern face softened, and he added, "And you'll be welcome. If you conquer the world, littlest brother, be sure to save us a piece." A last smile and a wink and Relan had been on his way. He knew that none of his family expected ever to see him again. One way or another, when someone left the high valley, they never seemed to come back.

But if they could see him now! Mail glinting in the sunlight, hair blowing in the wind and the heels of these magnificent boots ringing off the cobbles. Announcing to all the world that he who walked in these boots was not a man to be trifled with.

Yes, he would go back. Just as soon as he was finished, he would go back home and show them. All of them. His sullen family, the joyless villagers. He would go back like something out of the sagas the strange wandering minstrels sang in a vain attempt to cheer the flat, simple people of the land. But he would wait until he had something more than a new suit of clothes to show for his Adventures.

The farther Relan walked through the city, the more troubled his mood became. Everywhere he looked, he saw the signs of the last night's carnage. Blood spilled on the cobblestones, bodies lying in the streets. Loved ones gathering corpses. Families fleeing for the gates with possessions hastily piled in wagons. And fear on every face.

The music of his strides against the stones took on a sour note. He wondered if he should have done more last night. But the memory of what he had done, the creature and the killing of it, sent a shiver of fear up his spine. He hadn't had time to think. Hadn't had time to be afraid. But now that he had time, he was afraid, and worse. He was honest enough with himself to remember shaking afterwards. And the thought of going out into the night to face more of those snarling, tusked creatures on wolves–it turned his blood to water once again.

He should have done more to help. A real Hero would have fought all night. Would have fought until the enemy was driven from the city. But Relan had not. Why?

Perhaps because it wasn't his city? At least not yet. He had only been in Robrecht a week. And it hadn't been a pleasant week. Sleeping in a makeshift tent in a muddy ditch in the shadow of the south wall had been rugged enough. But the people were worse. Unfriendly, mean, shrewd, hard dealers one and all. None had the time to make a penniless Farm Boy feel welcome. For all the wonderful things he had heard about the cities, he couldn't understand why everyone was so excited about them.

He had almost given up. Then he had met Sabriella. She had appeared to him in the muck and the mire of Robrecht's agricultural market. Relan was on the verge of giving up. He had come to the farmers' stalls to look for work. He was a strong lad and knew how to work hard. But as he stood there, hungry, exhausted, covered in filth, somehow he couldn't bring himself to speak the words.

It would mean defeat. It would mean giving up and eventually going back to the farm in the tiny valley. It would mean that his brothers and sisters were right to laugh. And, worst of all, it would mean that the best he could hope to get from life would be that hard, beaten look that was the battered inheritance his parents had saved up for him.

"You seem troubled," a voice said.

Relan turned, and gasped. "What are you?" He was taken aback by a vision of perfumed breasts, full, lovely, and contoured under sacred robes.

"I am a Priestess, a loyal handmaiden of the Temple of Dar, but how could you not know that?"

"I, uh, am... uh..."

"You are a traveler!" she exclaimed, saving him from his awkward stammering. "A wanderer, a seeker of Adventure!"

"Yes," he said, because he would have said yes to anything this perfect, breathless woman said. She smiled, and Relan felt himself go weak in the knees. There was a gap between her front teeth that her tongue darted into and away from. She was the most beautiful thing he had ever seen.

"Dar commands us to serve all travelers and seekers," she said. "Tell me your name."

"Uh, Relan...?" he said, still bewildered.

"Well is it or isn't it?"

"What?"

She laughed brightly, in a way that was as far from mocking as the bright sunshine is from the rain. "Very well, Relan. I am Sabriella. I am pleased to meet you," she said with a curtsey. Then she slipped her hands around his arm and guided him from the marketplace.

"My, you are very strong," she exclaimed, accidentally telling the truth.

She guided him along Robrecht's streets until they were walking beside the nicest part of the river. The great keep loomed off to their right and almost managed, in the afternoon light, to look regal. Sabriella talked with him gently and gave him the gift of listening well and laughing often at his awkward stories. In no time at all, Relan was completely at ease with the radiant creature on his arm.

"Oh, but you must be famished!" she said, and dragged him into a small cookshop. The owner greeted her warmly, and they were soon seated. To her great delight, Relan had three bowls of stew. Best of all, the owner wouldn't take payment. Which was good, because Relan was completely broke.

They went back out in the street and walked for a time that felt to Relan like both an instant and an eternity. The sun cast longer and longer shadows through the narrow streets and alleys until finally they heard the tolling of the temple bell.

"But I must return," Sabrellia exclaimed, "I had not noticed the hours passing so quickly in your company. I have only been granted parole for the day, and the streets are not safe for such as I after dark."

"I will walk you to the temple and keep you safe," Relan said with all the sincerity there was in the world.

"You must not! I cannot be seen with you. And you cannot be seen with me. I know that to one so experienced in *Adventure*, the hardship of a dungeon and the Temple's Questioner mean nothing, but I am a much frailer creature."

"But, I don't think–"

She placed a finger on his lips. "You are so strong, so handsome, so brave. I know that if I were in trouble–in danger, I mean–you would come for me. That you would save me. Just like a Hero. My Hero."

He nodded like the idiot he was. And was going to follow her anyway, but then she paralyzed him with a kiss.

Of course, he had been kissed before. But the simple, sullen, load-bearing creatures of his village hardly seemed the same species as the delightful girl that pressed her painted lips to his. Such a kiss! He felt his feet break into a sweat. He closed his eyes and saw colors that he never imagined existed. It was the kind of kiss that would make a more experienced man ask some pretty hard questions about the purity of the Virgin Priestesses of Dar.

"Promise me you will meet me here tomorrow. Dar has inflamed me with love for you, and you cannot deny the Goddess her divine purpose. Say it! Say you will meet me."

He swallowed hard and said, "I will."

And then she ran off around the corner. As her sandaled feet slapped the cobblestones, Relan caught flashes of her milk white thighs beneath her flapping robe.

When she was out of sight, he rubbed his lips and smiled to himself. This was the start of it then. The grand Adventure of his life that he left the village to find.

Then the screaming started.

15

Relan rounded the corner so fast that he lost his footing and slipped on the cobbles. With the strength that came from long days of hard work on the farm, he caught himself on his palm and shoved the upper half of his body back into balance.

He saw two men in black running away with Sabriella, one holding her over his shoulder, the other glaring back at him and brandishing a wickedly curved knife. He was pretty sure *they* weren't priests of the infinitely kind and forgiving Dar, Goddess of Mercy.

On the street in front of him, a third man lay on the cobbles. He lifted a hand weakly and called after the kidnappers. "Please! Don't hurt her," he sobbed. Sobbed, thought Relan? What weak, unmanly, un-Heroic behavior was this? Had this man not heard the sagas? The full-throated minstrels singing of Heroes rescuing beautiful Ladies in Distress through Selfless Acts of Valor? This was not how it was done.

Clearly, this man would be no help. Relan dashed past him and turned the corner. In front of him was a long alley. Sabriella was nowhere to be seen. What sorcery was this? Relan ran faster, trusting in his belief that if a Hero was pure of heart, he would prevail in the end.

In defense of this naiveté, Relan had spent many of his formative years listening to the wandering minstrels who came to the village longhouse to coax a meal out of the flint-hearted farmers with Tales of Valor. He knew them all by heart. And in not a single one of them had the Hero ever stopped to check the doors he ran past.

Relan ran on and on, running out of patience before he ran out of breath. He trotted to a halt and spun around, glaring at the blameless buildings of old Robrecht Town as if they had personally wronged him. But, in the end, he was left with the ugly fact: they had gotten away with the Love of his young Life.

Cursing his luck and the perfidious sorcery with which Sabriella had been snatched away from him, he returned to where he had lost her. The wretched man was still sobbing in the middle of the street.

When he heard Relan's sandals, the man looked up and said, "She is my sister. Oh, cruel Gods, it is all my fault." He dropped his head, and his long, stringy hair fell across his face. Sobs shook his shoulders.

Relan picked the man up and set him on his feet. The wretch weighed almost nothing. "Who?" he asked. "Where?"

"It's all my fault," the man repeated. His large dark eyes seemed like haunted pits sunk into his pale skin. "The dice. I lost too much money at dice. And they have come for her."

Relan said, "I can rescue her!"

"You? You have money?"

"No, I have no money. But I have courage."

"Courage?" he said, gazing into a hopeless middle distance. "They won't take courage. I owe them money. Do you have money? Can you get money? I meant to get money at dice. But..." and here the pitiful sobbing took over once again.

"I can rescue her! If you would but tell me where they have taken her."

"No, they would kill her before they would let you have her. No, money is the only way. It is the only way to do anything in this world," the man with hopeless eyes said.

"Look at me. Look at me!" Relan commanded. "I will return your sister to you. This I vow. Now tell me, where they have taken her?"

"You?" said the man with a laugh bereft of hope. "You don't even have a sword."

The man's pitiful wails seemed to follow Relan through the streets as he went in search of a sword.

16

Of course, a sword was hard to find. Relan had tried to beg or borrow one for two days before he worked up the nerve to go and talk to Boltac. He had gone to the market again, looking for work as a laborer. He had begged for change from rich passersby. But nothing had worked. Sabriella's brother, a poor wretch named Stavro, lived in a shack built against the outside of the south wall. Every time he saw Relan, he wailed and cried. He told and retold his sad tale, claiming that it was all his own fault, but he would not *do* anything about it. He lacked the courage, he said. He lacked the strength, he said. All he had was Love for his sister and hatred for himself.

He was worthless, except for the information that Relan managed to extract from him. The men who had taken Sabriella worked for a thug named Hogarth, who controlled gambling in Robrecht. They had taken her to a hold in the south, a pile of dark stones on the river Swift known as the Tower of Forgetting. There they would keep her for a week. Then the rapes would start. The week after that, they would cut fingers off. Relan did not think to ask how this creature, Stavro, could describe such tortures in detail without breaking down into tears.

Relan, of course, vowed that he would rescue his lady (with all Faithfulness and Heroism) but the how of it had been impossible until he had saved the Merchant Boltac. Now that he was armed, free, and left to his own devices, the question became: what should he do? His lady had been kidnapped and wanted rescuing. He could think of no saga, song, or lay in which the Hero had left his lady in peril to embark on a larger, more important quest.

But, in a moment of unusually clear thinking, it seemed to Relan that the needs of the city should come before the needs of one heartbroken Hero. Shouldn't they? Robrecht must be avenged, and the threat of these Orcs and that flying Evil Wizard had to be dealt with. Clearly, that was a selfless Hero's first duty. Wasn't it?

So it was that, lost deep in the shallows of his limited philosophy, Relan bumped into a wheelbarrow with a corpse in it. He muttered half an apology before he recognized the man pushing the barrow. "Stavro! You have survived the assault. I am so glad." Relan heard a sharp intake of breath. A decidedly *feminine* intake of breath. He looked up to see a teary-eyed Sabriella on the other side of the wheelbarrow.

"Sabriella, you have been rescued!"

"Why, I uh, yes, Relow! I, uh, have been..." She looked from side to side, unsure of what she should say in this situation. Relan's smile faded when he realized that the man standing behind her was none other than the man in black with the knife who had carried her away from him in the first place.

"My lady," Relan said, "I thank the Gods that you have been returned to me unharmed, but I am confused by..."

"Oh, I just bet you are," one of the men in black quipped.

"Silence, varlet, or I will stave in your head," Relan said, because it seemed like the kind of thing a Hero should say in this situation.

"Let's steal his boots!" said the man in black, because it was the kind of thing a Thief should say in this situation. Relan answered by drawing his sword.

"Oh ho, ho. Look who's a man at arms now!" exclaimed the man in black, as he drew his wickedly curved dagger. "You'd best grease that up so it will hurt less when I take it away from you and stick it up your..."

"Whack!" said the man in black's skull as the pommel of Relan's sword came down on it.

"Please don't hurt me!" cried Stavro. "Haven't I been through enough?"

"You?" shrieked Sabriella, "What about me? How could you forsake your own sister, so recently rescued from ruffians of, uh, ill-intent!"

"Sister. You're not my sister! I swear, they forced me to do it. Please don't hurt me. Oh, Shirley, you sure know how to pick 'em. I thought he was just a country bumpkin. Did you see how fast he moved?"

"Wait," said Relan, feeling that he should have some part to play in all of this, "You know the men who kidnapped you?"

Stavro said, "Ah, *there* it is. You can take the bumpkin out of the country, but you can't take the–OH MY GODS, I take it back, please don't kill me."

"I haven't killed anyone... here," said Relan, "What happened to him in the 'barrow?"

"Torn apart, by those things," said Sabriella, "those Hork-Hork things. He died trying to protect me."

"Protect you!?!" cried Stavro. "We ran and you locked him out. I still remember him clawing at the door and screaming. Don't look at me that way, Shirl. This grift is blown, this town is done for, let's just bury Herveaux here and get on down the road."

"Shirley? Your name is Shirley?"

"Well, I see you two have a lot to talk about," said Stavro, "I'll just wheel poor Herv out the east gate, and when Thorvin wakes up you can catch up with–"

"NO!" Relan and Sabriella/Shirley shouted.

"Those things are coming back, you know," Stavro said ruefully. "It's not safe."

"I go to root out the source of this Evil," said Relan, not taking his wide eyes from Shirley.

"Then you're an idiot, kid," said Stavro.

"No, he's brave," said Shirley, not taking her eyes off of him.

"But I see it is not the only Evil that plagues Robrecht Town. Treacherous woman. I... I... Loved you."

"I know you did," said Shirley, not without kindness. "That's my gift. As for the rest," she shrugged, "don't blame me. It's the world that's treacherous; I'm just trying to keep up. Besides, a girl's gotta make a living, hasn't she? And I don't have a big, strong man like you to protect me." As she said this, she edged closer to Relan, unafraid of the naked blade in his hand. She pushed the flat of it gently out of the way with her fingertips.

"We were trying to take whatever money you could scrape together. I'm not proud of that." She ducked her head bashfully, then threw her hair back to reveal an expanse of perfect, pale throat that drew Relan downward into her dangerously plunging neckline. "But the feeling was real, you know." Then, like the sun breaking through the clouds after a storm, her pouty frown was replaced with a dazzling smile.

"Come with us!" she said. "We could journey the land together. Make money, have Adventures, share love—we could have it all. And with you I can finally ditch these losers."

"Right here," said Stavro, grunting as he struggled to push the unconscious Thorvin on top of the corpse already in the wheelbarrow.

Relan almost believed it. Shirley almost got away with it. But whether the Gods were looking out for Relan or Shirley's luck had run out, didn't matter. Relan caught a flash of morning sunlight as it glinted off the thin-bladed dagger Shirley was concealing along her wrist. It wasn't stout enough to chop off a limb, but it was thin enough to slip between chain mail rings, just far enough to tickle his heart and kill him.

"What are you going to do with that?" Relan asked. And then he did it right. He didn't give her time to explain. He didn't give her time to stab him. He hit the beautiful creature in her beautiful face with his fist. Then he looked down in horror at what he had done. A Hero never, ever hit a lady.

Relan ran away in shame.

When he heard the punch, Stavro had just finished getting Thorvin into the wheelbarrow. When Stavro turned and saw Shirley unconscious on the ground, he said, "Aw, come on!" He was already sick of this day.

As Relan ran north, he thought he might have just learned some kind of lesson. The confusion, the pain in his heart, the feeling of being totally inadequate to the moment–yes, that's what it always felt like when he'd learned a lesson before. But it wouldn't be until years later that he would be sure.

17

After Relan left the city, he followed wolf tracks north for the better part of the day. He ran to the point of exhaustion, trying to put the shame of hitting Sabriella, Shirley–whatever such a woman should be called–behind him. At the time, he had been certain that she was going to stab him. But now, he had doubts. Maybe she had just been scared. Relan knew he was scared, deep down, in that part of him that wasn't fit to be a Hero. But even if she had tried to kill him, a real Hero would have found a way to deal with it without hitting her.

All in all, Adventure wasn't turning out like he had expected, that was for sure. It wasn't excitement or Glory. More than anything, it was sore feet. The fine new boots that had looked so good in Boltac's store had started to gnaw at him as soon as he made it into the woods.

• • •

As the day wore on, Relan's self-criticism grew sharper, and his pace grew slower. Now he was spending more time resting than limping. Finally, he gave up on the boots, pulled them off, and tossed them in the heavy sack he alternately carried and dragged behind him. Even with feet blistered raw, it hurt less to walk barefoot.

And why not? He had gone barefoot in warm weather ever since he was a boy. The only boots he had ever known were animal hides wrapped around his legs with leather strips to protect him from the deep mountain snow. And today was good weather. A fine day, except for the memory of the sack of Robrecht haunting him. It was bad enough to see the burned-out husks and buildings, the common folk nursing their wounded and wrapping their dead in shrouds. But the memory of how that thing had felt dying on the other end of his sword was worse.

He had wanted a sword so badly. But now that he had one, it hung heavy on his hip, pulling him around to the left. After the day's walking, he could feel a pain in his left knee and hip. Every time his hand brushed the cold steel of the hilt he shuddered.

But he had saved a man's life! And the thing he had killed hadn't even been human. Then why did he still feel awful when he remembered how the Orc's rattling last breath had felt transmitted through the hilt of the sword? Didn't saving Boltac make him a Hero? Is this the way that Heroes were supposed to feel?

Relan wanted to give up. He had made little or no progress, other than punching a woman. But he kept going. If there was one thing he thought he knew about this business of Heroism, it was that Heroes didn't give up. Even when things got hard. No, Heroes pressed on. Saw it through to the bitter end. And sometimes, yes, even died Heroic deaths. But, was he a Hero? Or was he the other kind of man? The ones they didn't write songs about. The ones who took their boots off.

Relan hung his head and concentrated on putting one bare, calloused foot in front of the other. He didn't raise his head for a long time. Not even when he heard the rattle of a carriage and the heavy footfalls of draft horses on the road behind him. He just set his jaw and walked on, prepared to walk off the edge of the earth if that's what it took.

"Climb on, idiot," said a familiar voice.

Relan turned to see the Merchant, fat and happy, holding the reins of the Duke's Carriage.

"What? How?"

"Not only am I smart enough not to pick a shitty pair of boots. I'm also smart enough not to walk when I can ride."

"Unlike you, I am not running away."

"Sweetheart, you are clearly not running anywhere. At best, you're limping," said Boltac

"I mean, I go to face this dread foe who has so wounded our fair city. I mean not to flee, but to revenge this wrong."

"That's a lotta big fancy words. You want to be the big Hero? Save the girl, win the Kingdom, all that?"

"Yes."

"Well, that's where I'm going."

"You?" asked Relan, in danger of developing a healthy skepticism in light of recent events.

"I do have to warn you, you're probably not going to make it through this thing alive."

"Me? But I'm young and strong. You're old and fat. You're the one who's going to be killed first."

"En-henh. I'll give you odds on that. Out of the two of us, who looks more dangerous? Seriously, you got a crossbow, which one of us you gonna shoot first?"

Relan let the question sink in.

"You are young and strong and scary looking. They'll definitely shoot you first. Me, I'm non-threatening."

Relan still didn't climb onto the carriage. "What changed your mind? Isn't this what you pay taxes for?"

The smile dropped from Boltac's face. "The Duke ran away. Took his guards with him."

Relan's mouth dropped open. "Can he do that?"

"Age and treachery kid. That's his play, and it's a good one. For him at least. So it's just us. Ain't nobody else. Which is good, because what we are going to do is *very* dangerous and *very* stupid."

"It's not stupid. You're going to rescue the lady, the Love of your Life!" said Relan.

"Something like that. I mean, I eeeeeeeh... like having her around, and I'm going to get her back, but 'rescue' is maybe too strong a word to, uh..."

"Stout Merchant, from down here it looks like you are blushing."

"Oh, uh, it's just the heat. The sunshine, you see. I'm not used to it on account of I'm in my shop all the time," said Boltac, mopping at his face with his sleeve.

As Boltac covered his emotion, Relan climbed aboard the coach and sat beside Boltac. "True Love. It is a noble cause. I will lend you my sword, stout Merchant."

"You mean you're gonna lend me MY sword!"

"It's just a figure of speech," Relan muttered. Boltac hitched the reins, and the heavy draft horses lurched the carriage into motion.

"Ahh, I know kid," said Boltac. "You got a good heart, but you're kind of an idiot. No offense. I mean, think about this. What is in this for you?"

"Well, I'll get to make a name for myself. Be somebody. Maybe get a girl of my own."

"You know we're going to get killed, right? *You* are definitely going to get killed. And it's not even your girl."

Relan smiled. "Not if you brought any more of those healing potions. I mean that was amazing. I've never seen anything like that. I didn't even know–"

"Kid, I didn't bring any more potions. Not like that."

"Well, why not?"

"Because that was the only one I had. Magic, *real* Magic, is very expensive. And it's tricky. If a plan depends on Magic, it's probably not gonna work."

"But it was the most amazing, stupendous, unbelievable thing I have ever..."

"This is what I'm saying. It was *Magic*. But the downside is I'm probably growing an extra liver. Or a lung in the middle of my stomach."

"It worked out. You're alive."

"Yeah, so far it worked out, but next time, ennnh?" Boltac tipped his palm from side to side. "With Magic, there's always a catch. That's how they get you."

"So what did you bring?" Relan asked, looking at the bags on top of the coach.

"A little of this, a little of that, and a shitload of coin."

"Why money?"

"Why money? WHY MONEY?! Are you serious?"

"There's not going to be anything to buy."

"Are you kidding? There's gonna be all kinds of things to buy. Not least of which, the woman I want to get back."

"Wait, I thought this was a Daring Rescue!"

"No, it's just a rescue. If possible, I'd like to keep the 'daring' to a minimum."

"But how am I supposed to make a name for myself?"

"Easy. You lie."

"Lie? A true Hero would never do that."

"Okay, how many Heroes do you know kid?"

"Well there's Uthgar, and Frowen, and C'huhoyle..."

"C'huhoyle my squeaky wagon wheels! Not Heroes from sagas. Not dead guys you heard about in a song someplace. I mean, how many honest to Gods Heroes do you know? Had a beer with?"

"Uh..."

"Take your time. Make sure you count them all," Boltac said as he let the soothing clip clop of the horse's hooves and the tranquil beauty of the forest road lull him into a kind of trance.

"None," interrupted Relan.

"Did you miss any? I mean is that an exact count? Because, as a Merchant, I can tell you, it is important to be precise with figures."

"Okay, okay, you've made your point." Relan said, staring off into the trees.

"Yeah, that's what I thought. There are two possible reasons for this, and pay attention, because they are closely linked. One, everybody who sets out to be a Hero gets killed. And two, there's no such things as Heroes."

"That's not true. That can't be true! Why, there have to be Heroes. Who else would look out for the poor and the unfortunate?"

"The poor and the unfortunate either look out for themselves or... well, or they just keep being really poor and unfortunate."

"That's terrible. That's the most awful thing I've ever heard."

Boltac shrugged. "Hey, these are dark ages in which we live. I don't make the rules. I don't even like the rules."

"The rules suck. And I think you have it wrong."

"I wish I did," said Boltac, "but there's nothing either of us can do to change it."

They rode on in silence for a long time. Finally, Boltac grew so bored he decided to try again.

"Kid, do you know why people fight wars?"

"To win?"

"Nobody wins in a war, except the guy selling swords and armor. No, people fight wars to put themselves in a better negotiating position."

"Not for Love, or Honor, or a Righteous Cause?"

"Not in my experience."

"But in the songs..."

"Kid, they're songs. *Songs.* As in, not real."

"They're real to me."

"En-henh. And that's great, but the point here is that fighting is stupid. Negotiation is power."

"I don't think—"

"Yeah, I figured that one out already. Just trust me; if we can bribe our way in and out of this thing, everybody will be a lot happier. And a lot more alive. Hey kid, you mind taking the reins for a while? I'm still a little woozy from that potion."

"Woozy? But it was Magic!"

"Trust me, the hangover you get from Magic is the worst kind of hangover there is. I'm gonna sleep it off in the back. Don't go chasing after anybody while I'm asleep."

18

Rattick was no Hero. Like all true survivors, he always seemed to find ways to profit from the misfortune of others. So at the first sign of trouble, he slunk into the alleys of Robrecht. While Orcs marauded through the town and fire ravaged the buildings, he kept to the shadows, looting corpses where he could, burgling a store here and there, until finally he reached the north gate. He found a horse in the guard's stable and was gone into the night without a second thought.

When Rattick reached the forest, he abandoned the horse and worked his way along the road from twenty yards into the woods. When he grew tired, he climbed a tree, wrapped himself in his cloak, and tried to nap. His sleep did not last long, for he was awakened by the sounds of the raiding party returning from Robrecht. Horrible things on wolves crying "Hork, Hork, Hork!" as they rode the unlit roads. Rattick wondered what Treasure they had taken from the town. Probably just people, for food. But just in case, he followed their tracks, looking for dropped baubles by the light of a waning moon.

The raid was bad news for Robrecht, of course, but good news for Rattick. When word got out, Adventurers would come from all parts of the Four Kingdoms. They would see Glory, and loot. And with such a school of fish to draw from, Rattick's grift was about to go big time. Maybe he needed a partner to handle the additional volume? But the problem with taking a partner in a grift was how could you trust a grifter?

With his careful traveling habits, it took Rattick three days to return to the entrance of the Wizard's lair. And by that time, it wasn't there anymore. The once-grassy hill and innocuous-looking wooden door had been blown apart, leaving a smoking hole in the earth.

Wolf tracks led directly over the edge and into the maw of the pit. Evidently, the Wizard had had enough. It was not hard for Rattick to envision the scene. Often enough, he had heard the Wizard's howls of frustration echoing through lower dark of the dungeon. Of course, Rattick had been amazed and frightened by the mighty Magicks he had seen the Wizard work. But that's what made it funny now. That one so wise in the ways of power could be so ignorant of patience. That was amusing. And worth remembering.

Had someone made it past the Troll and stolen something of true value from the Wizard? Yes, that would do it. And Rattick wouldn't be surprised. His grift had been keeping the Troll so well-fed that half the time he brought Adventurers there, he'd had to wake the beast up to get him to eat his marks.

A theft certainly would have pushed the Wizard over the edge. His temper lost, raging against insults real and imagined, his foul creations scurrying for cover... yes, that must have been the way of it. The Wizard throws his hands into the air, says a word of power, and the entire hillside blows outward into the night. With a hue and cry, he lets slip the Orcs of War.

Yes, that's how it would have happened. Dimsbury had enough power to do it, that was for sure. He was a Wizard more powerful than any BattleMage Rattick had heard of.

It was the kind of scene one would place in a mighty saga to give the Hero time to rally an army and save the town. Except, there was no Hero. And there was no army. Just a wound in the earth and an unsuspecting town that had been sacked. And would be sacked again and again, now that it was defenseless.

So now he would wait for the next party of Adventurers. When they came, he would spin his sad Tale of Love and Life Lost in the fall of Robrecht. He would summon tears to his false eyes and tell how he had come for vengeance, but had realized that to attempt the depths of the fiendish dungeon alone would be surest suicide. Then he would promise to serve his new friends faithfully.

After a while, he grew tired of standing around waiting for the next flock of Heroic lambs. So he climbed into a tree, found a comfortable limb, and went to sleep. But his dreams of blood and fortune were soon interrupted by the sound of horses and, wait, was that a wagon?

He peered down through the leaves and spied a coach fit for a King. A King, or a party of Adventurers so rich that Rattick would only have to run his bloody con one last time before he retired to the warmth and debauchery of the Southron Kingdoms.

He jumped down from the tree so quickly he nearly broke his leg. As he rushed to greet the Adventurers, he saw that the strong-jawed blond lad who drove the carriage was wearing a very, very high grade of armor. A good sign, thought Rattick, expensive armor, even on the servants.

"Hello, hail and welcome, proud Adventurers. Be on your guard, for you have come to the lair of a Wizard most foul and dangerous. Humble as I am, I place at your service my unworthy person, Rattick." He finished with a low bow.

Before he could raise his head, he heard a familiar and irritating voice say, "Ah, Rattick! Do I have a deal for you!"

He snapped up from his bow. "BOLTAC!?"

19

"Rattick!" answered Boltac, not missing a beat. "Is it ever your lucky day!"

"Why?" asked Rattick with narrowing eyes.

"Like I said, I have a wonderful deal for you. A deal no *honest* man could pass up."

Rattick made a face. "I think that you are a long way from your store, shrewd Merchant."

"And don't I know it. Relan, unload the bags while I have a word with Rattick here."

"Who's he?" Rattick asked, nodding at the kid.

"Him? Oh, he's the Hero."

"If he's the Hero, what does that make you?"

"The cunning fat guy who outsmarts everybody in the end."

"I don't understand," said Rattick, telling the truth for once.

"Rattick, I want to hire you. Now before you protest, here's ten gold pieces, and there's more where that came from. Plenty more. I seek an audience with the Wizard at the bottom of this smoking hole, and I want you to get me there."

"I... I..." Rattick stammered to a halt. Between trying to twist circumstance to his advantage and trying to figure out what in the hell circumstance was up to, he locked up. Finally, he asked, "Have you lost your mind, fat Merchant?"

"What? You mean because I'm here? Yeah, probably. But I haven't lost my cunning, you understand. I'll give you half your reward now, half when you get me back to town."

"Twenty gold pieces is not enough."

"I know that, Rattick. I do. That was just to get your attention."

"I don't know if I..."

"Of course you can. What's that smell?"

"Troll."

"There's a Troll?" asked Relan, as he removed Boltac's bag from the carriage. "Is this all you packed?"

"I travel light," Boltac said, taking the sack from him. "If there's a Troll somewhere in this hole, it's the same Troll Rattick's been using to kill hapless Adventurers just like us. Isn't that right, Rattick?"

"I would never do such a thing. I am here to avenge my beloved Robrecht. And I, for one, am shocked, SHOCKED–"

"Yadda, yadda, yadda. See, kid, what he did there? Ahh, never mind. What he did was despicable, but the important thing is that we're not going to fall for it, are we?"

"No, we're not," said Relan, not knowing what he wasn't going to fall for. "Because I'm here to protect you."

"Protect me? Ha. Kid, you're here to carry the Lantern." Boltac reached into his bag and handed Relan the Magic Lantern of Lamptopolis. As soon as Relan touched it, it blazed forth with a brilliant light.

"We're not going to be sneaking up on anybody with that thing," observed Rattick.

"Eh, yeah," said Boltac, "you're right. You carry it."

"The Magic lamp," protested Relan. "Do you trust him with it?"

"I trust him to be totally untrustworthy. Consistency. I can work with consistency," said Boltac. As soon as Rattick took the lamp it went out. "Hmm. Smart lamp. Okay, we'll use torches."

Rattick handed the darkened lamp back to Boltac and asked, "What do you want with me, Boltac?"

"I want to make you rich. Name a figure, Rattick! How many coins do you need to guide me to the Wizard at the bottom of this smoking hole in the earth?"

"Why do you want to see him so bad?"

"He has a friend of mine. And I'd like her back."

"Ho, ho, ho. Is this Love? Love from the man who is all business?"

"Yeah, I'm all business; how much you want?"

"I can't get you past the Troll."

"What do you mean, Rattick? Sneaky little weasel like you?"

"No, no, I swear it. Ever since Dimsbury put the Troll there, even I haven't been able to sneak to the lower levels. Trolls have a very good sense of smell."

"Nah, you're just rotten to the core, so you stink to high heaven. But don't you worry about that. You get me to the Troll, and I'll take care of him."

"What? YOU? You can't be serious," Rattick collapsed in laughter.

Boltac frowned. "Y'know Rattick, if I'm gonna be your boss, you might want to show me a little respect."

"My boss? No offense, but I try not to work for people who will get me killed."

"Ah, so little faith. I tell you what." Boltac pulled a full coin purse from his belt. "This is for you. And three times this much when we get back to Robrecht with the girl."

"Even with my help, you don't stand a chance," said Rattick.

"Don't forget about me," said Relan drawing his sword. The conversation came to a complete halt as both men stared at the Farm Boy.

They stared so long that Relan became uncomfortable and asked, "What?"

"Put that away before you hurt yourself," said Boltac. "Now where were we?"

"You were just about to get yourself killed," said Rattick.

"Ah yes, exactly, ye of little faith. I tell you what, Rattick. You lead me to the Troll, and if I can't defeat your Troll, you keep the gold. I mean after the Troll eats me and shits it out."

"Trolls shit gold?" asked Relan, very confused.

"Gold is very hard to digest. Isn't that right Rattick?"

"I shall do as you ask. Then I will loot your corpse with great relish."

"There he is. There's that guy I know and distrust. C'mon Relan. Let's go meet the Troll."

20

As they descended into the darkness, Rattick thought about knifing them both then and there. They wouldn't be expecting it. It would be a quick, certain profit. Perhaps less than he might expect, but there would be no chance of getting killed on Boltac's foolish quest. No sooner had the thought crossed his mind than Boltac said, "I know what you're thinking, Rattick: 'Why don't I knife these two right now and go through their pockets for loose change?'"

"That's not *exactly* what I'm thinking."

"Yeah, but close enough. And you want to know what I'm thinking about? Other than your inevitable and predictable betrayal?" Rattick was silent. Boltac continued, "I'm thinking, if you're our guide, you should be going first. Kid, give this slippery bastard the torch."

"But I'm one of your key suppliers!" protested Rattick

"He's going to run off and steal the torch," said Relan, displaying the first glimmers of wisdom.

"Nah," said Boltac, "if he steals it from me, he won't have anybody to sell it back to. But if he makes you nervous, go ahead and poke him with your sword a little bit. Don't kill him, just make him leak."

"Shh," said Rattick.

"'Shh' yourself, you crooked bastard," said Boltac.

"What's that noise?" asked Relan. In the distance, they could hear a horrible rumbling noise.

As they approached, the noise came and went in waves. It sounded like someone gigantic trying to exhale through a set of lungs filled with gravel. It was a horrible, igneopulmonary rumble.

"That's the Troll," said Rattick.

"Doing *what*?" asked Relan.

Rattick waited until after the sound had rumbled through the corridor again.

"Snoring," whispered Rattick into the silence. "Which is a good thing for you, stout Merchant. What I suggest is that you keep to the shadows. Advance only while it's snoring. Then you take your sword and plunge it right in his ear. It's one of the only vulnerable places on a Troll."

"I don't have a sword," said Boltac.

"You can use mine," offered Relan.

"That's nice of you, kid. 'Cause after all, it's my sword. But I'm not going to need it."

"What are you going to do?" asked Rattick.

In the flickering torchlight, Boltac took his heavy wool mittens from his bag. As he put them on he said, "I'm gonna do what I do best. I'm going to make a deal with him."

Relan searched his memories for any sagas or songs in which the Hero had defeated the monster by making a deal. He came up empty.

Rattick asked the obvious question. "Have you ever seen a Troll?"

21

The Troll was asleep next to a mound of phosphorescent lichen. Strictly speaking, the creature didn't need light to see, but the presence of this slight illumination allowed the Troll to see the terror on his meals' faces more clearly. There is an old Troll proverb that says *"food better frightened"* or *"scared is good eatin'"* or *"terror is the best sauce."* It loses pretty much everything in the translation. But in case there's any confusion on the matter, Trolls aren't nice.

Something kicked the Troll in the foot. This was a new sensation for the Troll. There really isn't anything in nature in the habit of kicking Trolls. The Troll opened his large, yellow eyes. In the dim light of the lichen, he could clearly see food, holding a small sack and looking up at him.

"Yoo-hoo, Mister Trooooooolll. Have I got a deal for you!" said the food.

Wait, food was talking? This was confusing. Food never talked. Sometimes food screamed. Sometimes food tried to poke the Troll with sharp things. Most of the time food ran away. But it never stood its ground and talked. And certainly never kicked. Since the Troll couldn't understand what any of the funny, squeaky little sounds coming out of food's mouth meant, it tried to understand *why* food wasn't doing any of the things that it usually did.

Maybe it was poisoned? That thought disturbed the Troll. Since he often ate people without bothering to peel them, his stomach was a cause of constant trouble. He had been eating quite well lately. For some reason, food had been easier to come by—eager even—since he had come to this cave. He didn't even have to go out and terrorize the countryside just to get lunch. But how had he gotten here? He couldn't remember that part. Something about a very loud and angry piece of food wearing black. But the memory was blurry and confused.

Thinking made the Troll's head hurt. He decided that he had thought enough for one day. He drew himself up to his full height and yawned. A Troll yawn is much like a roar, and this one was so loud it rattled chips of rock off the ceiling. The Troll expected food to flee, or curl up in a convenient, bite-sized ball of fear, but food was still there!

"There we go," said Boltac, "Come get a closer look at the merchandise."

In the shadows, Relan said, "He's dead."

A Rattick-shaped shadow next to him said, "You are not as dumb as you look, kid."

"Thank–" Relan began.

Rattick pressed a finger to his lips and silenced him. "Shh. Don't ruin it. I'm going to enjoy this," said Rattick.

The Troll lowered his head and made two whuffing grunts. This expulsion of air freed his tusks from the ponderous folds of his cheeks and filled the enclosed space with the foul stench of Troll breath. He stepped forward to begin his charge.

"Here," said Boltac, "Try this." From within his sack of holding, Boltac produced a glittering silver mace. The head was encrusted with jewels that glittered in the uncertain light of the dungeon. The whole thing was so large that it was more decorative club than mace proper. He held it out to the Troll and said, "Just try it, see how you like the heft."

The Troll, not being smart enough to fear a shrewd Merchant's smile–and well-accustomed to not understanding what was going on–took the relatively tiny mace in his absolutely gigantic hand.

"There," said Boltac, and he released the mace. No sooner did let go of the bejeweled head of the weapon than the Troll was pressed to the rough stone floor as if he had been smashed there by the hand of an angry god.

22

Pinned to the floor, the Troll seemed much less fierce. His eyes were wide, and shifted fearfully as he whimpered a little. His foul claw remained tightly wrapped around the ornate mace.

"What is that?" asked Rattick.

"That is a very cursed Mace of Encumbrance," said Boltac as he removed his mittens.

"Magic," whispered Relan.

"Yeah, kid, that's Magic for you, there's always a catch."

"Like dealing with you," Rattick said to Boltac with newfound respect.

"Hey, I didn't force him to do anything. 'Here you go Mr. Troll. Here's a free mace.' He took it."

"But the Troll didn't know..." said Relan.

"That's there's no such thing as a free mace? Everyone knows this. That's how they get you. And that's especially how they get you with Magic."

"But what about Wizards? They use Magic," countered Rattick.

"They always end up doing themselves in. Just 'cause you get away with something for a while doesn't make it safe."

Rattick said, "Awed as I am by your cunning, good Merchant, one question remains: How did you learn about the mace?"

"A guy brought it in a carrying case and refused to take it out. I thought maybe I could get the jewels off, but the enchantment was too powerful. My last apprentice was pinned to the floor of my shop for a week before we figured out how to get him out from under that thing."

"How did you manage it?" asked Rattick

"Ahhhh," said Boltac, holding the thick wool mittens up in the air. "Woolen Gauntlets of Magic Negation. Very rare, very powerful, and very handy."

"They look more like mittens," said Relan.

"Yeah, basically. But Gauntlets have a better ring. Merchandising. You tellin' me you're gonna pay top dollar for Magic mittens? So, let that be a lesson to both of you. Stay outta my bag. No telling what you'll find in there."

"No problem," said Relan.

Problem, thought Rattick. He didn't know what could possibly be in Boltac's Magic bag, but now he knew for certain that it was Magic. There was no way a bag that size could contain such a big, heavy mace. It had to be Magic. Why, the bag itself, never mind the contents, had to be worth more than even he could imagine. And that was saying something. Rattick had quite an imagination where riches were concerned.

"C'mon, I don't want to be all day getting my lady friend back," said Boltac as he headed into the darkness. "How deep do you think this goes anyway?"

All the way to the bottom, thought Rattick.

23

The faint light from torches and braziers flickered throughout the round room as if it were afraid of being caught there. The space had been carved from the living rock, but, in a concession to the occupant, mortar lines had been chiseled into the stone to create the illusion that this room had been constructed by masons. If one ignored the lack of windows, one might well imagine that this was a room in a tower, keep, or castle, instead of hundreds of feet below ground.

The room had a high, arching ceiling, with a hole in the top. The smoke from the burning coal and torches sent streams of greasy smoke into this upper darkness. Below, thick rugs, the fine work of Southron craftsmen, divided the room into several areas.

In the very center of the room was a round hole, six feet across, capped by a wooden cover. On the left was a collection of shelves filled with scrolls, codexes, potions, and ingredients under glass.

On the far side of the room was a raised dais with a kind of altar. On the altar was a large glass jar, perhaps half the height of a man. In the jar, a flame danced, but it seemed to be just out of focus. Its weak light threw strange shadows and shapes on the wall behind it, but its light did not penetrate any farther into the chamber.

And on the right, at a desk covered with papers and oddments, sat the Wizard Dimsbury, slumped in frustration. The heels of his hands pressed into his forehead, he scowled from beneath his troubled brow at the mountain of paperwork before him.

The Wizard had prided himself on his ability to create and control monsters. But in his quest for power and understanding, Alston Dimsbury had inadvertently created a monster so powerful and unruly even he couldn't control it. This savage beast was known as an Organization. And a hungry beast it was, demanding a never-ending flow of supplies, inventories, requisitions, orders–attention of every kind. Some 2,000 Orcs and wolves required feeding and clothing and organizing. It was all so *tedious*. He had needed an army, so he created the Orcs. Now what he needed was an army of smarter Orcs to keep things running. But smarter Orcs were a problem.

Intelligence is a dangerous thing to breed into a creature. You could never know which way it would go. Too much intelligence, too much initiative, and your creations would be rebellious and impossible to command. Too little intelligence and they would be useless, sometimes dying because they forgot to breathe. It was a lesson Dimsbury had learned the hard way.

In all his experiments with the various strains and cultivars of the species "Orc" (his own name, and he was quite proud of it) Dimsbury had had many, many failures. But he could only count one unqualified success in his quest to create the perfect mix between intelligence and servility. He was so pleased with this Orc he had given it a human name: Samga.

Once Dimsbury saw how useful Samga could be, he made it the overseer of all the other Orcs. In a short time, Samga had become his right-hand almost-man.

Samga approached the desk with a covered tray. Dimsbury looked up and said, "Ah, lunch." At last, a reprieve from paperwork. Samga smiled, or as close to it an Orc could manage, and set the tray down.

When the Wizard lifted the cover, he found a gory, unappetizing mess. He struggled to read what was on the plate before him. It looked like two slices of bread, some lettuce, two slices of tomato, and a lot of bloody meat. The Wizard gently asked, "What is this?"

"It's an M.L.T.," grunted Samga with all the manners and polite inflection he could muster. "Man, Lettuce and Tomato samwich."

"And what is that?" asked Dimsbury, pointing at one of the more disgusting bits.

"Well, it's either Man, Lettuce, or Tomato." Seeing the foul look on the Wizard's already foul-looking face, Samga quickly changed tack, "O' course, the finest sliced leg of man."

"Raw leg of man, I assume?"

"Oh, of course, my Master. Only the best for you."

The Wizard replaced the cover on the vile lunch-like creation that sat before him. "And the leg of man is, I am to understand, uncooked?"

"Oh, of course, my–oh, I see what you're getting at. It's just that Orcs don't, you know, cook meat, so the cooks don't, uh..." Samga seemed genuinely hurt and flustered. "Really more butchers, then, aren't they?"

"There, there Samga. Your kind was not bred for cuisine. I understand. Simply take it away and bring me the female prisoner."

"You want us to cook her?"

"No, Samga. I have other uses for her. Bring her to me unharmed."

"Oh, all right," Samga said with obvious disappointment. He hunched over the tray and shuffled towards the door, tusks hanging low.

"Here, Samga, what's wrong now?"

"Nothing, my Lord. It's just, she looks *delicious*."

"Yes, Samga, she certainly does."

24

After the Wizard had flown off with her, Asarah had managed to scream for all of twenty seconds before she passed out. When she awoke, she found herself unharmed in a cell of damp grey rock. There was no window and no furniture.

Next to the pile of straw where she lay was a candle burning in defiance of the oppressive dark of the cell. By its feeble light, she could see that the only way in or out of the room was a heavy wooden door with a small opening.

Through the opening, she could see that the hallway beyond seemed to be carved out of the same rock as the cell. She listened carefully but heard nothing. When she moved the candle away from the window, she thought she could see the merest hint of a flickering light from the other end of the passage.

"Hey!" she yelled. There was no response.

"You out there! I know you're out there. You can't have a jail without a jailer!" She heard the scraping of a chair against the stone floor. "Come here! I need to see you. I demand to see you!"

The unknown jailer made a shuffling, snuffling noise as he drew nearer. She could hear him but couldn't see him. What manner of man didn't use a light? She held the candle out of the opening to get a better look.

A face of grey-green, leathery skin, punctuated by tusks and beady black eyes, came at her from out of the darkness. It snarled, and Asarah jumped backwards and dropped her candle. It sputtered and went out before she could pick it up again.

There, in the terrible darkness, she heard herself sob and realized how afraid she truly was. She could hear the thing breathing on the other side of the door. She prayed she wouldn't hear the sound of the door opening.

Eventually the thing grunted and walked back down the hallway. Asarah did not cry out again.

She felt her way back to the straw and curled up in a ball. This was awful. This was worse than anything she had ever imagined. To be in a cell was one thing. But to be trapped in a cell because you were afraid to attempt escape...

After what felt like an eternity of terror in the darkness, she heard steps approaching again. And this time light came with them. In spite of herself, her hopes rose. Perhaps this would be a person–a human being–rather than that awful thing she had just been subjected to. She looked to the faint glimmer of light that came through the doorway, but she did not rush to the opening.

Another of those strange, monstrous faces thrust itself forward, but instead of grunting or snarling, this one spoke a soft, strangely accented English.

"Pardon, my lady, but The Master would like to see you now."

"The Master?" asked Asarah, reassured by the creature's kindly demeanor. "Who is The Master? For that matter, who are you? And what manner of hospitality is this?"

"I am Samga, my lady. And The Master is, well, The Master, maker of us all. And he has asked for you, the woman in his power." Ah, yes. Now it made sense to Asarah. The man who took her into the air had abducted her for a reason, the oldest reason of all. Men, thought Asarah: no matter how rich or powerful they might be, they were all the same.

"And what are you, Samga?" Asarah asked as she rose to her feet.

"I am an Orc."

"An Orc. And what is that?"

"I know not. None of us do. We are made, not born, in the bowels of the earth to serve The Master."

Gah, what an existence, though Asarah. And she simply *hated* the word 'bowels.' The door to the cell creaked open, and Samga entered. As she saw him in the full light of the lantern, he was less terrifying than she thought. It helped that he wasn't riding a wolf or sacking the town in which she lived. "So what does your Master want with me?" Asarah asked with a false pout.

"It's not wise for me to ask, my lady. We must go."

"Wait," said Asarah, "I must look a fright. Your Master will be unhappy if I do not have time to compose myself."

"The Master is usually unhappy," Samga said with a sad look that seemed out of place on a monster.

Asarah knew what the flying man wanted with her. She wasn't about to let him get the upper hand without a fight. And there were many ways to fight. Where a man had desire, a woman had the opportunity to torture. She took stock of her appearance as best she could without a mirror. Her hair, unruly at the best of times, was now an utterly out-of-control mess. That was okay. Some men preferred her that way. Unless she missed her mark, this Wizard was one of them. But her dress? Ugh. It simply wouldn't do. She smiled an evil smile and started ripping.

After her first few tears, her left sleeve and blouse were in tatters, revealing the hollow of her clavicle, most of her left breast and all of her left arm. Then she grabbed hold of the skirt below the knees. A few sharp jerks and she was showing a lot more leg. Then she rolled her lips inward and bit down on them hard to bring a bright redness to them.

There, she thought, that ought to put him in a twist. Not all men are Wizards, but all Wizards are men. Asarah, girl, we're going to see how much we can lead this one around.

Then she turned and tried it out on the creature. A toss of the hair, a full smile, a subtle roll of her hips. It should have hit him pretty hard, but she got no reaction from him. She asked, "What manner of man are you?"

"Samga is an Orc! Now come. The Master is waiting."

Hunh, she thought. Orcs must be gay.

25

Rattick led Boltac and Relan deeper into the dungeon. Sometimes they moved through natural caverns with stalactites and stalagmites. Sometimes they walked through abandoned mine works. But as they descended deeper and deeper, the quality of the workmanship changed. When they plunged into the bedrock, the tunnels seemed more organic. More gnawed than carved. It was in one of these strange, unsettling passages that they came to a fork in the passage. Rattick stopped and said nothing.

"Which way do we go?" asked Boltac.

Relan put his hand on his sword hilt. "I say we go right, stout Companions."

"Left," hissed Rattick in an immediate and automatic contradiction.

Boltac rolled his eyes.

"We should go right," Relan said, nodding to himself as if he was just figuring this out for the first time, "because the Right and Good is the... "

From a distance came the sounds of scraping footfalls and hissing grunts. These noises echoed wildly in the strange passages, so it was impossible to know if they were coming from ahead of them or behind. As they listened, the noises became louder.

Relan's eyes grew wide and he crouched down with a hand on his sword hilt. His gaze shifted quickly from passageway to passageway to passageway, but he could not look at all three directions at once. Boltac shook his head and looked to Rattick.

Rattick said, "Orcs, my Merchant friend. They infest the depths. And they hunger for the fatty flesh of shopkeepers, no doubt."

Boltac said, "Enh-henh. Let's keep moving. Quietly." Then he turned to Relan, "And if it's possible, don't do anything too stupid." He slapped his kid's hand away from his sword.

"To the right then, because we are for Good," said Relan, nodding as if the matter were settled.

"For Good?" snorted Rattick. "We are sneaking into a powerful Wizard's dungeon to steal from him, what's Good about that? You'll be no kind of thief at all if you try to be polite about it," Rattick said.

As the young lad's face grew red with anger, Boltac stepped between the two of them and asked, "Why do you want to go left?"

Rattick smiled, "I just like the left."

More guttural utterances echoed through the system of tunnels.

"We can't stay here," hissed Rattick, "too dangerous." Boltac made his decision by shoving through both of them and walking into the left tunnel.

Relan rushed after the Merchant, "But you can't trust him."

"I don't," said Boltac, "This tunnel leads down, and we needed to make a decision."

"He is not a Man of Honor," protested Relan.

"Kid, you don't know this yet, but Men of Honor aren't really all that useful. In particular, they make especially bad thieves."

"He means to lead us into a trap and steal the contents of your precious bag," Relan said.

"The bag is more precious than the contents... hey, wait a minute. Where is that weasely son-of-a-bitch?" Before they could turn back, they heard the sounds of a scuffle behind them.

"Ah, Gah, ah-Hah!" they heard Rattick say from around the corner. On the wall, they saw grotesque shadows, cast by torchlight, grab at the cowled shadow of Rattick. Boltac and Relan froze at the spectacle before them. There were hisses and grunts, muffled curses and the sound of thudding blows. Rattick cried, "Save yourselves! I will hold them as long as I can!"

"We should help him," said Relan.

"En-henh. You think he would help you?" Boltac said, already turning to run. Relan gripped his sword. For a moment, he was trapped there. Torn between the desire to do the right thing, and his certain knowledge that Rattick was an evil man. He watched the shadows tear at each other. Then he turned and ran.

When he caught up with the wheezing, slow-moving Boltac, the Merchant was already struggling under the weight of his brown sack. Boltac looked at Relan and struggled to say, "If you feel raw about it kid, you can try and rescue him later."

Relan ran ahead, thinking that he was being drawn into danger as the moth is drawn to the candle flame. Yes, maybe this was it. Maybe this was his chance to be Heroic.

The corridor bent at a right angle; Relan skidded to a stop. The stone work was more finished in this part of the cave system. The rough edges had been broken off and, here and there, there was evidence of polishing and brickwork. It gave Relan the impression they were getting somewhere.

He held up a hand so Boltac wouldn't run past him. But when he looked back he realized how silly the gesture was. Boltac was limping down the corridor, panting heavily and dragging his sack behind him. When he saw that Relan was looking at him, he nodded weakly and raised a hand.

Relan drew his blade carefully, not making a sound. Then he peeked around the corner very slowly. His jaw dropped. He retreated back into the passage.

"Pssst," Relan said as he waved frantically to Boltac, "Hurry!"

"Ennnnnn-heh," said Boltac, as he put on all the hurry of which he was capable. By the time he caught up, Boltac was panting so heavily that Relan was afraid it would give them away.

"Shhhhhh!" said Relan.

"Kid. I... ain't... made... for running," said Boltac between gasps.

"Look!" Relan commanded. Boltac raised his weary head, and they both peered around the corner. This time it was Boltac's turn to drop his jaw.

He had thought they were in a large space before, but when he saw the massive passageway around the corner, Boltac realized how wrong he had been. Here, underground, was a thoroughfare wider than any street in Robrecht. It looked to have been hewn from the living rock itself. Large interlocking arches graced the ceiling and descended in a series of columns that punctuated the center of the corridor.

Through this gigantic passage, Orcs walked up and down the angled passage, leading wagons as they traveled. On the far side of the passage, Boltac could see that the tiny hallway they were in continued on. Between them and the other side was a space five wagons wide, filled with Orcs. But these were not the snarling, ravening, bloodthirsty creatures that had descended on Robrecht. These Orcs looked positively... industrious?

"What are they doing?" Boltac wondered aloud.

On one side, a steady stream of Orcs descended in well-gruntled, torch-carrying groups of two or three. Closer to them, the crack of a whip and straining grunts announced the approach of a heavily laden wagon. Boltac and Relan retreated into the shadows of the passage. From the corridor below, a team of four Orcs, yoked like oxen, came into view pulling a crude wagon up the slope behind them.

The wagon was filled with raw ore of some kind. By the light of its foul, pitch-smoldering torches, Boltac and Relan could see that a fifth Orc sat on the cargo with a whip.

Crack! Went the whip. "Horrrrrk!" complained one of the haulers. And the wagon rolled on.

As the back of the wagon disappeared up the passage, Relan said, "If only..."

"Forget it kid, we gotta find another way."

"But there are so many of them... did you know there would be so many?"

"What, you thought this was going to be easy? I told you we were probably going to be killed. So quit your whining. Let's go back the way we came."

"We should go home," said Relan.

"What happened to the brave Adventurer?" asked Boltac.

"I can't kill so many. I, I, I, I..."

"C'mere for a minute."

"Go back? But what if we run into some of those things?" said Relan, fear freezing him on the spot.

"Orcs?"

"Yeah, Orcs."

"Well, there's a lot more of them out there then there are behind us."

Relan swallowed and his face went pale.

"C'mon, cheer up. You're gonna get another chance to be a Hero. Most likely, more chances than you want." Boltac turned back. He threw his torch down and stomped it out against the floor. From his sack, he produced the Magic Lamp of Lamptopolis. As he touched the lamp, it began to glow; Relan thought it seemed brighter than before. Boltac drew the shutter on the lamp until only the barest bit of light was spilling out. "Quietly now," he said.

As they made their way back down the hallway, Boltac spotted a small side passage that had not been visible when they came from the other direction. It was cut into the rock, leading away from the main tunnel at a 45 degree angle.

When he heard the shuffling, hissing noise coming from in front of them, Boltac didn't have to think twice. He turned towards the small passage saying, "C'mon, this way."

Relan didn't argue.

26

Asarah followed Samga out of the dark cell. The passageway outside was just tall enough that Samga could walk with the tips of his pointy ears just brushing the ceiling, but Asarah had to duck to follow. After a short distance, the passageway opened up into a larger cavern. This larger cavern revealed itself to be a tunnel. As they headed upwards, she could see many other tunnels leading off in all directions.

She was soon distracted from underground geography by the large number of Orcs moving through the passage. Some carried picks and shovels, others crates and barrels, and one pair of the creatures carried a third who had obviously been hurt. As they crossed to the center of the passage she could see a steady stream of wagons, each pulled by a team of Orcs. Full ones headed up. Empty ones headed down. What were they mining?

Even though all of the Orcs gave her the same unnatural, unpleasant stare, after a while they seemed perfectly normal to Asarah. She noticed that all the Orcs had slightly different colorations; like brutish snowflakes, no two were alike. Their snarls, barks, and grunts did not become attractive, but she was shocked to find that she was becoming accustomed to them. How could a whole new species have a life below the ground that no one knew of?

A small knot of Orcs walked past holding a log, lashings, and quite a lot of firewood. Other than the wagons, this was the only wood Asarah had seen down here. What did they need it for? And how far down were they, anyway? She had so many questions. She tried one of them on Samga: "What's going on?" she asked, gesturing to the wood.

For a few steps, Samga didn't answer. The more-grey-than-green of his back hunched a little as he shuffled his way through the tunnels.

Samga spoke, but he didn't slow or turn back. She hurried alongside him so she could hear his words.

"Adventurers. Trespassers. They killed The Master's favorite Troll. The Master doesn't know about it, but when he finds out, he will insist that they be roasted on spits. I do not want to be roasted on a spit also, so I have ordered the spits prepared for roasting early."

"Roasting?" Asarah asked, trying not to wince.

"The Master doesn't like raw meat."

"He is a cannibal?"

"What does 'cannibal' mean?" asked Samga.

"He eats people."

"No, The Master is a *good* Master! He gives the people to us. 'Course, we like them raw, but The Master must have his fun."

Asarah didn't ask any more questions. They came to a large arch in a formation of granite. In the arch was a huge door flanked by gigantic torches. Samga did not knock but opened the door and held it, waiting for Asarah to walk through.

When she did, Samga said, "Master, I have brought the girl."

From behind his desk, Dimsbury shot a foul look across the room. Banishing her tattered appearance from her mind, Asarah smiled. She had come a long way since her girlish days. The endless toil of keeping an inn had cut lines into her face, more from laughter than from frowns, but they betrayed her age. Even so, she was still very attractive. In some ways, more attractive than she had been as a girl. She hoped that his would be enough.

"Do you like my accommodations?" Dimsbury asked, still looking at her intently.

Asarah scanned the clutter of the round room. It was certainly the nicest decorated cave she had ever seen, but it was still a cave. Her eye was drawn to the disturbing-looking flame that danced in a gigantic glass receptacle. She didn't like looking at it, but somehow she couldn't look away. It was every color and no color at the same time. It flickered and danced, and seemed always just slightly out of focus. As she stared at it, she became queasy.

"You are a brave woman to stare so boldly into my flame. There are not many who can tolerate the sight of it for so long," said Dimsbury, stepping out from behind the desk and moving to stand close behind Asarah.

Asarah forced herself to keep looking at the eerie flame. She asked, "What is it?"

"What isn't it? That is the better question. It is the source, the power that binds and fuels all Magic."

"Is such power dangerous?" she asked, thinking that she was playing to his vanity.

"In the wrong hands, power is always dangerous."

"There is a more powerful Magic than this," she said.

"And what is that?" the Wizard asked.

"The force which draws Man to Woman," said Asarah, turning to face him and lean her ample bosom towards him as if it were an offering or a weapon. "You are a," she paused and bit her bottom lip, "*powerful* man. You take what you want. And you have taken me. Because you need a beautiful woman to bring comfort and pleasure to your life."

"Is that right?" Dimsbury asked, not pulling away.

"And you are afraid..."

Dimsbury snorted in disgust.

Asarah moved closer and continued, "...afraid that I will fear you because of your great power."

"You don't fear me?" Dimsbury asked with an air of bemusement.

"No. The force which draws a Woman to a Man is stronger than fear." She leaned in to kiss him. Her full red lips moving in an approximation of hunger. Closer. Closer. Until, in the last millimeter, Dimsbury erupted in laughter. The torrent of his foul breath poured into her face as if he were a sewer.

Asarah recoiled in shock. Was everything in this dungeon gay?

"You think that... excuse me," Dimsbury struggled to repress some very undignified giggles. Then he sighed and looked around for someone to share the joke with. But there was no one. "You cannot be serious."

"I am as serious as I am beautiful," Asarah said, almost choking on her own disgust for her words. But she had turned it over and over in her mind. Seducing this man was her only chance of getting out of this alive.

"I mean the thought of it! Really, it is too much."

"Isn't it?" she said, flashing a great deal of leg through her torn dress and hating herself for it.

"No, no, I mean, the very idea! You are a *serving girl*, an entirely different species from one such as I. The idea," he barked another laugh, "that I–I? A scion of a noble house could take as consort something like *you*? It is laughable, really. You are to me as," he indicated the parade of heads that adorned the wall behind his desk, "well, as I said, a creation, or another species. We could no more mate than could an eagle and a, a, a snail!"

Confused and not a little offended, Asarah asked, "Well, if you don't want to *ravish* me, then why have you brought me here?"

"It was not to shatter your Princess fantasy, I assure you. I have brought you here to be my *cook*," said the Wizard.

Asarah stood with her mouth hanging open so long that the Wizard felt he must clarify things for the simpler mind in the room. "Sandwiches, dear lady, I have brought you here to make me sandwiches."

"Sandwiches? You think I'm making you SANDWICHES!?" said Asarah with the fury of a woman who thought she had wanted to be scorned, but had just changed her mind. "I AM NOT A SERVANT!"

The Wizard looked at her for a moment. Then he gave her a smile that was anything but reassuring.

"I am glad you said that," said Dimsbury.

"Because now you see that I am no servant or serf?"

"Well, now we have the question out in the open, at least."

"It's not a question. I am no servant. I was mistress of my own inn and free house before you burned it to the ground."

"Yes, I am sorry about that. I am fond of the occasional overly flamboyant gesture, you know. But let us put the past behind us and start anew."

Asarah looked at him skeptically but said, "Ooookay. Try me."

"You call me a Wizard. And so I am," he indicated his surroundings. "As you can see I am a Master of Arcane and Powerful Forces, the workings of which you cannot possibly hope to understand. But, you are a clever girl..."

Asarah winced. He said "clever girl" in the tone of voice one might use to praise a prize horse or a well-trained dog. If this jackass was trying the smooth talk, it wasn't working.

Dimsbury charged on heedless of the effect he was having. "So, I believe you can understand the importance of my work here. Work that, if you chose to join the team, you would be supporting in a vital, culinary role."

"You see, I am not merely the cliché of some maladjusted character living in the bowels of the earth twisted and bent on revenge. Nor am I a mere conjuror,"–and here he threw up a burst of flame into the center of the room—"although revenge and conjuring are well within my capabilities.

"I am a creator, a researcher, a man who delves deeply into the very fabric that binds our realities together."

You're a guy who certainly likes to talk about yourself, Asarah thought.

"And I am father, to my awkward children. Isn't that right, Samga?"

"Of course," Samga said.

"Father? Of all of these... these?"

"Orcs, I call them. Yes, I made them. All of them."

"What are they?"

"An alchemy of fungi, mineral, and pure Magic. Things made, not born. And surprisingly faithful servants. They are my greatest work, to date." He gestured to the wall above his desk. Asarah realized that the heads mounted in a semicircle were, indeed, Orcs. It was a sequence, moving from Dimsbury's crude and puny first attempts, to brutishly strong examples, to a head that looked very much like the creatures she had seen in the halls. But at the far right, there was an empty mounting plate.

"What's the empty one for?" asked Asarah.

"Oh, that's for Samga. Someday, he will go there. He is my finest work, almost like a son to me."

Asarah looked at Samga. This revelation didn't seem to bother him in the slightest. Of course, Samga was an Orc, a horrible thing, but Asarah felt a moment of pity for him all the same. She turned back to Dimsbury and said, "Yeah. Son. I can see the resemblance."

"Really? How strange, we look nothing alike. You are a curious creature. Now that you have some sense of the importance of my work, let us talk about the terms of your employ."

Asarah drew in a breath and was just about to give the Wizard a furious piece of her mind when there was a pounding at the door.

"Come!" said Dimsbury.

27

An Orc charged into the room. This creature was squatter and more brutish than Samga, as if a giant sculptor's thumb had slipped and pressed the clay of him into an awkward wad.

"Master," it grunted. "Troll down."

"What?" said Dimsbury.

The Orc gave the Orc-ish version of a shrug and said, "Down. No get up."

"You mean *dead*?"

"No, down."

"Samga, would you please?" Dimsbury asked, with an annoyed wave of his hand. Samga conversed with the Orc in their shared, brutal tongue.

Dimsbury rolled his eyes and said to Asarah, "I am sorry about this interruption. There are always more administrative tasks wasting my time. Details, meddling Adventurers. And Samga is the only one of them who has any intelligence..."

Samga had more than intelligence. He had cunning. He had been very careful not to be the one to deliver the bad news about the Troll to The Master. He knew Dimsbury for the violent and tempestuous man he was. Especially when he was not pleased. And this news would not please him.

All Orcs could talk after a fashion, but Samga was the only one who could talk that The Master had not vented his fury upon. This was because Samga was very, very careful about what he said.

"Master," began Samga, "This one says the Troll in the upper passages has been killed. He tells me that there are three Adventurers loose in the lower levels."

"The TROLL! BLAST AND SLAPDASH!" Dimsbury roared. "Have you any idea..." he started to say to the Orcs. "No, of course not. You have no idea. You haven't a thought in your head. You are merely a stomach with legs that walks around making bad choices. My finest creation to date, indeed."

Dimsbury turned to Asarah and lowered his voice. "Have you," he began again, "any idea how hard it is to even find a Troll? Weeks away from work. Finding one, rendering the great big brute unconscious, having him transported here–tremendous expense of time and effort–and now someone has had the temerity to kill my Troll. I ask you, where am I going to get another Troll? At this hour? I don't have time for this! I don't have time for any of this!"

He pointed at the Orc and hooked his fingers so that his hand formed a ragged, palsied, fist-like object. The Orc writhed in pain as, inside its body, its bones were ground together by the unspeakable, sinister forces of the Wizard's Evil Magic.

When the Orc whimpered, Dimsbury smiled. Then the corners of his mouth dropped, and he sucked air in between his teeth. As he did this, the Orc's skin tightened, causing the creature's eyes to bulge out as if they were about to explode.

Asarah recoiled in terror from the Wizard's unspeakable cruelty.

"Oh no, my dear, you mustn't worry. They don't feel pain. Not really. Not any more than a machine or animal does." There was a terrible juicy crunching noise. Asarah looked away and screamed. She heard a wet slap as what was left of the Orc hit the stone floor. She couldn't help herself; shaking, she turned to look at the remnants of that poor creature. A low, wheezing moan rose from the fleshy pile on the floor.

"Dispose of this one, Samga. It is defective," said Dimsbury.

Samga nodded. With one arm, he reached down and removed the heavy wooden cover from the floor in the center of the room. Then, with a clawed foot, he kicked the crushed and still wheezing Orc in to the blackness of the pit.

Dimsbury said, "Creation is a messy business. One makes a great many mistakes, you see. But thankfully, I have a very deep pit in which to bury my failures."

In the silence that followed the word 'failures,' Asarah could hear the crushed corpse of the poor Orc still bouncing off the sides of the pit far below. Each time, the report of it was fainter and fainter.

Dimsbury answered the unspoken question, "Bottomless."

Samga dragged the heavy cover back into place.

"Samga?"

"Yes, Master."

"Send out patrols. Catch them. Bring them to me."

"They might get a bit killed during the catching, my Lord," cautioned Samga.

"Whatever is left, you bring it to me. And then? We will have them roasted on spits in the main hall."

"The Orcs won't like that, Master. Spoils the flavor of the meat."

"So I am told, Samga, but let that be a punishment for letting these dilettantes through in the first place."

Samga nodded and turned to go. "Wait," commanded Dimsbury, turning his attention on the wide-eyed Asarah, who was still staring at the pit in the center of the room.

"You. Yes," Dimsbury snapped his fingers, "Yoo-hoo."

Asarah looked at him the way a frightened rabbit looks at a fox.

"Have you changed your mind about entering my employ?"

Asarah trembled while she shook her head no.

"Really? Even after what you have just seen?" Dimsbury asked, more fascinated than upset.

Again, Asarah shook her head. Dimsbury's eyes darkened, and Asarah knew in her heart that she was going to be crushed and tossed in the pit like the butcher's scraps.

Dimsbury waved a hand in dismissal. "Oh, very well. Samga, chain her to that table over there. Perhaps boredom will change her mind. And give her some rags so she can clean up the blood on the floor. Excuse me, you stubborn woman, I must return to my work. Be quiet, and I won't have to waste my time killing you."

28

As soon as Boltac and Relan left the main passageway, the tunnel they were following sloped sharply up, then down. As they pressed on it twisted to the right, and then back to the left, as if the creatures that had made it couldn't make up their mind which way they really wanted to go.

When they came to a split in the tunnel Boltac went to the left. "You're going left?" protested Relan.

"Shaddap," said Boltac. Three steps in, the tunnel bent sharply to the left, dropped three feet, and split again. This time Boltac went to the right.

"Are you happy now?" asked Boltac.

"Shh," said Relan.

"Never mind the melodrama, let's keep moving," said Boltac.

"But what if they are following us?"

"Then we shouldn't make ourselves easy to catch," said Boltac, quickening his pace. But no sooner had he turned the corner than he came to another forking passageway. This time a passage led off to the right and just a few steps further, they could see it split yet again.

Boltac didn't break stride as he went to the left again, just to piss Relan off. This tunnel rose steeply and twisted to the right, above the original passage, then dropped into another junction that looked suspiciously like that the one that they had just come from, but that couldn't be possible.

"Ennh," said Boltac.

"We're in a maze," said Relan.

"No, we're not, we're just fine, I know right where we are," said Boltac, not managing to convince himself or his young Companion. The Merchant turned around and led them back the way they had come, but after three turns, they found themselves back in the same room. Or one that looked exactly like it.

"We're in a maze of twisty passages..." said Relan.

"...all alike," finished Boltac. He unslung the sack from his shoulder.

"What are you doing?" said Relan. "We've got to keep moving."

"I'm checking something," said Boltac, digging around in his sack. "Besides, if all these passages are alike, then it doesn't matter where we are."

"Unless we're being stalked."

"Ah ha!" Boltac lifted the Magic-detecting wand from the bag. He waved it up and down in the air and then held it in each of the four exits. The wand did not react.

"What?"

"This maze of little twisty passages is just a twisty little maze of passages. It's not Magic."

"So? We're still lost."

"Yeah, we're lost, but we're not completely screwed. A solution exists," said Boltac holding up his finger.

"And that is?"

"Let's try always taking the right-most passage." Relan agreed to this and they set off. They walked for what seemed an eternity, but every junction they came to looked the same as the one they had come from. After an unknowable number of intersections, Boltac muttered, "Twisty maze of little passages." He said it like the curse that it was.

Relan sat down roughly and half said, half sobbed, "It's no use. We're lost."

"Easy kid," said Boltac, "It's an Adventure. It never goes according to plan."

"PLAN!" exploded Relan. "WHAT PLAN?"

"Shhhh!" said Boltac. "We don't know where we are. But more importantly, we don't know where they are." He sat down next to the young man and said, "We'll rest here for a minute, get our spirits back."

He reached into his Bag of Holding and produced a skin of water and some dried meat. He drank some water and passed it to Relan. Relan swallowed greedily and wiped his chin off with his tunic.

For a while, they sat chewing the dried meat. Finally, Boltac said, "Okay, kid, I get that *I'm* an idiot for doing this but, not for nothing, what are you doing here?"

"I want to be a Hero."

"Yeah, but why? I mean, before, I'd sooner die than be forced to listen to your story, but since we're probably going to die down here anyway..." Boltac said with a smile.

"Why are you so cheery about it?"

"You don't know nuttin, kid? This is an Adventure. Of course, my favorite Adventures are trading expeditions, but same thing. And the First Rule of Adventures is: They're always miserable. If you expect that–if you expect the worst–then you have a much better time of it."

"You mean like my feet and those boots?" Relan said, wiggling his bruised and battered toes.

"Ah, that's nothing. Once, we got enveloped in a dust storm coming out of Shatnapur. The winds blew for three days. We had no idea where we were going. Even the damned camels got lost. We were out of water for three days before we found an oasis. Hell, oasis, that's being generous, it was a puddle of muddy water. Some of the camels wouldn't even drink from it. But I drank. Felt fine for about an hour. Then I shit myself all the way to the next well. Eh, it was awful. My camel went from sand colored to Boltac's Bowels Brown. Terrible."

"That's awful."

"That's Adventure. Why d'ya think I own a store?"

"Because you're old and fat and mean."

"I wasn't always old and fat, y'know. And someday, if you're very, very lucky, you'll be old and fat like me. And you might not mind so much."

"Not me," said Relan, "I'm out to make a name for myself."

Boltac stretched his legs out in front of him, and lowered the shutter on the Lantern so that a faint red glow filled the room. The Merchant stared into the gloom for a long time. Then he said, "Once, long before you were born, I carried a sword for a living. From far to the north. I first came to Robrecht from Mercia. To conquer the wilds and make a name for myself."

"But you don't look Mercian."

"I'm not. Not exactly. My tribe is, well, we're scattered. My family traded in the Mercian Empire, but weren't exactly citizens, you see. So my dream was... well, same as your dream. I was going to go out in the world and prove myself to be strong and brave. Make a name for myself. Earn the token of citizenship. And then... and then I don't know what.

"My father thought I was an idiot. And it took me years to realize he was right. The day I mustered out for that long march south, he said, 'Boltac, you're a trader, a Merchant, it is in your blood. Someday, remember it and learn to be happy.'

"I told him I was going to be a soldier and make him proud. His eyes filled with tears when he told me that killing would never make him proud. That I should be a Merchant, keep a store, raise a family, know something of life before I died. Add something to the ledger of the world, rather than take, take, take.

"I don't remember exactly, but I suppose I said something much like you did. Called him old and fat, probably called him a coward... ehhh. He was a lotta things, my old man, but he wasn't a coward." Boltac shook his head and looked away for a long time. "Anyway, I never saw my father again. I came south. I think I imagined we would conquer the Southron Kingdoms single-handedly. There were four of us in the 7th Repreitors. We were thick as thieves and twice as greedy.

"Athos, he was a scout. And far south of here, just coming out of the mountains, he was scouting wide on the left flank of the army. And he came across an ancient city, crumbling on the edge of the jungle. Of course, there was no one there. But there was the promise of riches. The untold riches of an ancient civilization. You don't have to be a Merchant's son to do the math on that one.

"We bribed the lieutenant. I was a supply sergeant, so I got us what we needed. And off we rode, bold as Heroes."

"Did you find riches, powerful weapons, jewels?" asked Relan, his eyes wide with greed and Glory.

"What we found was jewel-encrusted death. I was the only one who made it out alive. I lifted a terrible sword from a funeral bier, and as soon as I drew it, the sword attacked. Not me though. The cursed thing welded itself to my hand and went after my Companions. Within minutes, they were all dead, and I was alive."

"It wasn't my fault, but I never forgave myself. Of course, I couldn't go back, not with all of them dead. So I deserted. Six months later I heard that the army had been destroyed, broken against the White Walls of Yorn. So I came to Robrecht, which wasn't under the Mercian Empire at that point and, well, the rest, as they say... "

Even as he said this, Boltac recognized that it wasn't the whole truth, but it was as much of the truth as he was willing to tell.

"What happened to the sword?" asked Relan.

"I carried the awful thing with me in my travels. Thinking that the power and the skill of the sword would make me a mighty robber. It saved my life with some bandits, but in the end the screams, the memories of the faces of the men I had killed, especially my comrades in arms–who had become my family after I abandoned my own–I couldn't bear the touch of the thing.

"I threw it in the deepest part of the river Swift, and I have not drawn a sword since that day. And, to tell you the truth, I don't care if I never draw one again."

"After you kill the Wizard you mean?"

"I don't want to kill anybody."

"But he is a terrible man!"

"Fine, you kill him."

Relan thought on this a while and said, "With such a powerful sword, you could have been a King."

"Nah, kid. They don't let guys like me be King. Not even in fairy tales do guys like me get to be King."

"Why? Can't anybody be a King?"

"You gotta better shot of being King than I do. Farm Boy turns out to be a prince, that's a great story. Merchant? Nah, that never happens. Not in a million years, kid. And y'know–"

Boltac put a finger to his lips and looked up sharply. Relan heard it: something moving through the tunnel. The sound of strange, scraping footfalls and a hissing. In the passageway they had just come through they could see the flickering orange glow of torchlight. It grew brighter and brighter. Something was tracking them.

Boltac whispered, "Draw your sword. This is where you get to be a Hero."

"What?" whispered Relan.

"Listen," said Boltac, "Here's how we're going to do this."

29

Hissglarg smelled human. And orders were very clear about humans. They were to be eaten. Not the crunchy face-parts, no, no. Those were to be saved for identification, of course. But all the rest was fair game. Like all Orcs, Hissglarg loved human meat. Of course, he had been bred to.

It was a silly trait, one that evolution would never have put up with. All Orcs really needed to survive was a constant diet of the deep minerals they had been grown from. But when Alston Dimsbury set out to do a job of *Evil* Wizarding, he didn't leave it half done. No matter what they needed to live, Alston had decided that his Orcs would have a proper lust for the flesh of mankind. What did he care for the delicate processes that formed the natural world?

This was all well and good (especially for Dimsbury's vanity) but human meat played hell on an Orc's digestion. In fact, nothing about an Orc's digestion was very good. A single Orc, left to its own devices, could eat rock and soil all day yet fail to extract enough nutrition to survive. And so this odd, created species dug and quarried and filtered and smelted and refined. They excavated vast underground complexes, not for pretty jewels or shiny metals, but for dinner.

Hissglarg held the barely sputtering torch close the ceiling and sniffed the air. Yes, this time to the left. He sucked the air and scuttled forward. Strictly speaking, Hissglarg didn't need light. Born and raised underground, the feeling of the rock under his claws and the scents of minerals, warren-mates, and intruders were all he needed to navigate his way through the most tortuous of underground passages. He could never get lost. He would just follow his own smell back the way he had come.

Orcs carried the torches because of something the-one-who-spoke-the-human-tongue had told them. Hissglarg couldn't remember the exact words right now, especially with the intoxicating smell of meat so close. It was something about humans liking light, that if they were lost in the dark they would come right toward it. (It was close enough, what Samga had told his fellow Orcs was, "Keep the light in their eyes. They are easier to catch that way.")

As he stepped out into the junction, he thought he saw something move to his left. But he when he turned to look at it, brilliant light flooded the passageway. It was so brilliant he thought it was that most abhorred of things, the sun. But what would the sun be doing underground? Hissglarg covered his eyes and cried out in pain. Then he threw his sputtering torch at the source of light. The light faded. In the returning darkness, he saw a fat sack of human meat scrambling along the ground after a lantern. Ah, dinner! thought Hissglarg.

The entree on the ground turned and looked behind Hissglarg. Its eyes went wide and it shouted something in the meat-tongue. Hissglarg did not understand what it said, but he looked behind him anyway. And there, to his surprise, was more meat. This one held a sword in its shaking hand. It was younger and thinner than the one on the ground. In fact, it looked kind of stringy. But Hissglarg would eat the sword too. Metal was tasty and good for you. The Orc grabbed the shaking metal blade in one of his taloned hands. Tears streamed down the boy's face, but he did not run.

Then there was a thud-clink and blackness closed in from around the edges of Hissglarg's vision. The Orc collapsed to the floor unconscious.

Relan blinked the tears back from his eyes and saw Boltac standing over the collapsed Orc with a heavy coin purse in his right hand.

"Why didn't you stab him?" Boltac demanded.

"What did you hit him with?" Relan asked, still shaking and trying to change the subject.

"Money. About 150 gold pieces. Mightier than the sword," Boltac said with a wink.

30

After she was shackled, Asarah crawled under the table and lay down. She did not cry. She did not give up. But, when the rage and the adrenaline shivered out of her, she grew tired.

She struggled to stay awake, to observe her surroundings and her captor carefully, to find a weak link in her chain, a soft spot in the wood of the table, or any flicker of distraction that she could use against the Wizard. But there was none. After Samga had left, Dimsbury had turned his back on her and devoted his full attention to the out-of-focus flame on the other side of the chamber.

She had watched him for about 15 minutes before the chanting started. It was low and guttural, and sounded like the Wizard was speaking with more than one voice. The sound of it seemed to come from behind her. But when she whirled around, there was only the curving stone wall of the spherical chamber, catching the echoes and playing tricks on her.

The effect of the strange humming/singing noise coming from the Wizard's throat, the stench of a smoldering brazier in the corner, and the hypnotic flickering of the in-focus/out-of-focus flame/non-flame trapped under a cylinder of blown glass all conspired to put her to sleep.

When Asarah awoke, she could not have said if minutes had passed, or days. She heard voices. When she opened her eyes, she saw that the strange flame under glass was brighter now, and in better focus. The fingers of eerie light it cast throughout the room were more substantial, carved deeper shadows. On the far side of the room, two of the shadows were talking.

Dimsbury towered over a cowled figure standing in the deepest shadows. The two of them spoke in whispers. She couldn't make out any of what they said, until the Wizard stood up straight and exclaimed, "What? Come to rescue... the *cook*? You must be joking."

The smaller figure shook his head and murmured more intently. When he paused, the Wizard said, "Ho, ho, ho, no. Really? That is rich. Yes, yes. No, wait: bring them here. Making an example of them will be a pleasant diversion."

"Yes," continued the Wizard, after another pause, "of course there will be a reward. I presume someone like you does nothing out of the goodness of your heart."

The shadow turned and left the room. Try as she might, Asarah could not see the cloaked figure's face, but his walk was familiar. Strangely familiar. Her curiosity and her natural impudence overcame her self-preservation.

"Who was that?"

"What, oh? I forgot you were there. I find your question tiresome, so you should sleep," said the Wizard. With a wave of his hand, he rendered Asarah unconscious again.

31

Relan looked at the unconscious Orc and said, "I am a failure as a Hero."

"You'll get no argument from me," said Boltac. "But don't feel bad. Most Heroes are. Now what do we do about this?" he said, gesturing at the Orc.

"Kill him?"

"Me or you, Mr. Hero?"

Relan flinched a little at this. Boltac's expression softened and he scratched the side of his round face. "Well, figure they already know we're here. And one more Orc won't make much of a difference."

"But, you must kill him, Boltac, you must!" said Relan with great sincerity.

"En-henh. Well, if it's so important to you, why don't you take my sword off your hip and cut him down." Boltac looked down at the Orc. As it slept, its terrible features somehow took on an innocence. When Relan did not speak, Boltac said, "Yeah, that's what I thought. Tie him tight, we'll leave him."

"But how are we going to get out? It's a maze Boltac. A maze!" whined Relan.

Boltac slapped Relan across the face. "Now, you listen to me. I didn't ask you to come. In fact, I told you not to come. I told you you'd probably get killed, right?"

Relan nodded, rubbing the red mark on his face.

"And are you killed yet?"

Relan stood there, still breathing.

"Then cheer up, 'cause things could be a whole lot worse. And likely will be before we're done. You wanted an Adventure, ya big dumb ox, and you got one. So now what are you gonna do?"

Relan didn't say anything, but knelt down and began binding the Orc with strips of leather that he cut from its jerkin.

Boltac stuck his belly out and stretched a good long stretch. "Okay," he said to himself. "Now that we're good and screwed, how do we renegotiate this deal?"

"May I suggest stealth?" whispered Rattick's voice from the shadows.

"You sneaky bastard," exclaimed Boltac, "you're alive!"

"Yes, I am rather less dead than my enemies would like. This is the truth of it."

"How did you survive?" Relan asked.

"The Gods love a thief," said Rattick.

"You know, Rattick," said Boltac, looking directly into the shadow where he thought Rattick was, "as your employer, I have to tell you, I have some serious questions to ask you. Not the least of which is, why didn't you tell me there were so many of these things?" he asked, gesturing towards the Orc.

Rattick stepped out of the shadow behind Boltac and said, "To be honest, I did not think you would survive this long."

To Boltac's credit, he didn't jump... much. "En-henh, so now what?"

"For all the gold you have, I can return you and the boy to the surface where you will be safe."

"I didn't come this far to return home empty-handed."

"You wish to go on?" Rattick asked, his thick eyebrows expressing surprise.

"En-henh."

"You, perhaps," said Rattick, "but I don't think the youngling is still so keen."

"My courage is as good as yours, sir."

Rattick unwrapped his cape of faded black. He stood toe-to-toe with Relan and looked up into his eyes. "I am no sir,"–he looked the lad up and down in a way that made his next word a curse–"sir. And what does that make of your courage?"

"Test me and you will find me ready, sir," said Relan, trying to make an insult of his own. But the quaver in his voice was less than convincing.

"Very well," said Rattick, giving Boltac a mocking bow, "I lead where my Master commands."

"What'sa plan, Rattick?"

Rattick bent down and lifted the Orc's tunic. He plunged his dagger into the soft part of the Orc's thigh and held the creature's garment away from the spurt of greenish-black blood. The Orc let out a soft, sinking moan, as if it was deflating into death. The blood pulsed slower and slower until finally Rattick said, "There, now you can untie it. Bring me its clothes."

Relan was wide-eyed and pale. He looked to Boltac. Boltac just observed everything with a look of professional disgust. As if the whole thing were going to cost him money no matter what he did. Relan bent to the task.

"I know these passages far better than I have let on, stout Merchant." Rattick said, as he wiped his dagger clean with a black rag.

"No shit, Rattick? You've been keeping secrets from me?" Boltac asked with absolutely no air of surprise.

"You have no idea."

"En-henh. So, once again, what'sa plan?"

"By keeping to the shadows and whispering with their ancient tongue, I have found the woman. She is being kept by the Wizard in a room at the very bottom of this dungeon."

"You found her, and you didn't bring her back with you?"

"Gods, no!" hissed Rattick. "She is clumsy and loud like you. And how I am I to know that she would not do something stupid, like this one?" He pointed at Relan. "For money, I risk my skin, but for nothing do I risk my life."

"A wise policy, Rattick, and one I support. But can you get us to her?"

"I can, but you will have to do what I say, when I say it," he pointed at Relan, "Especially you. If you do not, I will slit your throat myself."

"I'd like to see you try," said Relan.

"That's the point," Rattick said, his eyes floating glassily in the feeble light of the winding darkness, "you wouldn't see me try. You wouldn't see me at all."

"All right, all right, Mr. Death-Waits-in-the-Friggin-Darkness, you're very scary–do you have a plan or not?"

"I do," said Rattick, "but you won't like it." Then he stripped the crude clothing from the Orc. When he was done, he said, "Now we must skin him."

"Skin him!" said Relan.

"I told you you weren't going to like it."

32

It hadn't taken that long to skin the Orc, Relan thought, not really. It just felt like forever because he had wanted to throw up. Relan had skinned things before, sure. Deer, squirrel, pig. But never a person. Orcs weren't people. They were monsters, but they had faces that were just too human.

Boltac shook his head and turned away while Rattick worked with his sharp knife and little tugs and jerks. "You really think *this* is going to work?" asked Boltac. "What's your plan, scare them to death?"

"Scare, no," said Rattick, "distract and confuse."

"With a pinch of disgust thrown in for good measure, no doubt," added Boltac.

"Ah, there it is." Rattick held up the skin and scalp of the dead Orc, complete with ears. He had fitted the creature's faceleather to his hand and held up the dismal beast's countenance, as if it were a puppet. "Looks like you," Rattick said to Relan. Then he darted his hand towards Relan's face and made him jump. The ragged cackle that followed was the first time Relan had heard the evil little man laugh.

"I don't trust him," Relan said to Boltac.

"I don't trust him either. I *employ* him," said Boltac.

Rattick donned the Orcs crude harness and then slipped the creatures face and ears over his own.

"Wait a minute? Where did Rattick go? He was here just a minute ago," said Boltac. "Seriously, that's a disguise?"

"This is a distraction."

"Where are our disguises?" asked Relan.

"They're never going to see you."

"I'm not much on sneaking around like a coward," said Relan.

"Oh, you won't be *sneaking*. You don't have the talent. They'll just be looking elsewhere."

"What?"

"C'mon kid, I think I know what he means. Rattick, get us out of this maze before the Orc starts to rot."

Rattick bowed low, "Your humble employee lives to be of service."

• • •

They retraced their steps to the main tunnel. If anything, there were more Orcs than before.

"Horrrrrrrrrrrrrrr, horrrrrrrrr," the Orcs wheezed as their powerful legs pushed against the crudely paved surface of the tunnel. Slowly, slowly the wagons climbed from the depths.

"Merchant," asked Rattick, "do you have any oil in that remarkable sack of yours?"

"En-henh, just a minute." Boltac rummaged through his bottomless sack.

"There are so many of them," said Relan.

"So many shadows in the darkness, and what will three more be?"

"Is that from a saga? It sounds like it's from one of the sagas," asked Relan.

"No lad," said Rattick from the darkness, "it's not from a song of Heroes, but from a song of the other kind."

"There we go," said Boltac as he pulled a large flagon of oil from the depths of his Magic sack.

Rattick took the flagon and said to Relan, "Heroes aren't the only ones who perform deeds worth singing about, youngling. Watch and learn."

Rattick wrapped himself in the Orc's skin and donned his cloak of darkness, seeming to disappear before their very eyes. A shadow moving through shadows, he stepped into the flow of traffic. He was a blackness with pointed ears, nothing more. For a moment, he was in step with the wagons going up, and then he stepped into the lee of one of the great pillars that kept the ceiling from collapsing.

If Relan hadn't known better, he would have thought this was just another Orc resting on the long climb to the surface. And if he hadn't known better he would have thought that this ordinary Orc was relieving himself on the pillar? Rattick held the oil flagon at his crotch and poured it out onto the passage floor.

"Uh, is he..?"

"Clever, I'll give him that."

"In front of everybody?" asked Relan.

"Hidden in plain sight. Our friend is very, very sneaky. No wonder he's stayed alive so long."

"He's not my friend," said Relan.

As wagon neared the pillar, Orc-Rattick appeared to finish his business, looking like just another Orc in the darkness.

The next wagon was pulled by six Orcs, yoked together in teams of two. As the pair closest to the wagon drew abreast of the pillar, something happened to one of the Orcs. It barked out in pain and dropped in its traces. The other Orcs immediately bellowed in rage, as the "driver," lashed out with the whip indiscriminately. The cavern was filled with such a roaring and commotion, Relan couldn't hear himself think. Even though Relan was looking for Rattick, he almost missed the sneak-thief's next move.

A ripple of darker darkness came across the floor, underneath the reins of the wagon. It was Rattick, rolling with noiseless precision. There was a small, silver flash in the murk and another Orc collapsed, clutching a wounded leg. The roars of protest turned to howls of fear as the wagon slipped backwards. The driver whipped and whipped, but it was a disaster in slow-motion, the oil making it impossible for the remaining Orcs to keep their footing.

The driver was on to Rattick. He saw a figure that was not quite Orc, crouching motionless on the floor. Relan tensed to flee. But as the driver cried, "HOARRRRRRRK!" and raised his whip, Rattick uncoiled from the floor. He grabbed a torch from the holder on the front of the wagon and shoved it in the driver's face. As the Orc screamed in agony, Rattick continued the motion, lofting the torch into the river of oil he had poured onto the floor. As it erupted in flame, Relan could see Rattick rolling towards them across the floor.

Flames engulfed the wagon team. The overloaded wagon slid backwards, crushed the Orcs behind it, and slammed into the next wagon. A terrible cry went up as the entire train of carts broke loose and crashed into the depths, one after another.

The flames died down quickly leaving Relan barely able to see in the darkness. He was only aware of the sounds of agony and the smell of burning flesh. "It's horrible," Relan said.

"That guy is worth every penny," said Boltac.

"NOW!" Rattick hissed, appearing between them as if from nowhere. He thrust both of them across the passage and into the mass of confused Orcs. Some were trying to flee the flames. Others were rushing to help their fallen comrades. They were everywhere, pressing on all sides of them.

"Keep moving," Rattick hissed.

Relan was nearly overpowered by their oppressive, musky scent. He wondered if this was what a lathered horse must smell like in hell. If any one of the Orcs in the passage had looked closer they would have recognized them for human interlopers they were. But, in the confusion, the Orcs did not see them. The three were across the passage and safely away into the darkness. Relan felt like laughing. They had gotten away with it!

33

Asarah was awakened by someone shaking her shoulder. She shrieked, and scrambled back underneath the table.

"It's okay, it's okay, it's me," said a voice that was familiar but shouldn't have been there. Asarah opened her eyes and saw a face lit from underneath by a faint glow. She gasped. The figure opened the shutter on the lamp it held and more light flooded out into the room. It overpowered the otherworldly glow of the sinister flame under glass so that she could see who it was.

"Boltac?!"

"The one and only."

"What are you doing here?"

"What am *I* doing here? What are *you* doing here. You're the one who got us into this mess."

"Us? Wait, what's going on?"

"I'm here to–"

"No! No, you are not. Are you telling me that I'm the damsel in distress? I am NOT a DAMN DAMSEL in DISTRESS!"

"Fine, fine," said Boltac, "just keep your voice down. Now, how about you rescue me and get out of here."

"That's right! Because I'm the Heroine. I am the girl who rescues herself."

"And doesn't forget to take her best customer, Boltac, with her."

"Best customer, ha! Why, Boltac, when you're not trying to chisel me out of a drink you're trying to beat the check."

"En-henh, and I'm very sorry about that, but if you could hurry up and rescue me so we could get out of here..."

"Oh," said Asarah, sighing into the darkness, "I forgot. I'm chained to this table."

"Ah."

"Yeah."

"So, uh, if I..."

"Don't you even think about it," Asarah said.

"Well, I think I have something in my sack here that could loosen those chains enough so that, y'know, you and I..."

"All by ourselves? You attempted this stupid rescue all by yourself—what were you thinking?"

"Hurry up!" Relan whispered from across the darkened room.

"Wait, you brought someone else on this suicide mission?"

"Ennnn...yeah, the kid I loaned the sword to?"

"You're endangering a *child* in this foolish rescue attempt?!"

"All right, enough!" Boltac yelled, his voice echoing through the chamber.

"I think somebody heard that," whispered Relan.

Boltac clapped a hand across his face and shook his head. "Look, Asarah. Please be quiet."

"Quiet!" she shouted, "Why should I be quiet? So you and some other fool can get himself killed in a rescue attempt that is pointless, because I was going to save munh..."

Boltac smothered her mouth with a kiss. It was so unexpected that when it was over, neither of them knew what to say.

Asarah spoke first. "Uh?"

"You know this already, but I never told you. I love... I Love you."

"The only thing you love is money, Boltac," she said.

Boltac ignored this and plowed on. "And here's something else you already know. You should shut up and let people help you."

"Hmmpfh."

"En-henh. That ain't an argument."

"Hm-*mpfh*!" she said, making it into an argument by sheer force of inflection.

"Okay, look. If it makes you feel better, I didn't come here to rescue you. I came here to ransom you. You know, to buy you back."

"BUY ME!" screamed Asarah, creating a racket that might have been louder than any racket this dungeon had yet heard. "THAT'S EVEN WORSE!"

From the darkness, there was laughter. In keeping with tradition, laughter from darkness should be sardonic. Or sinister. Or, at the very least, mocking. This laughter was not. This laughter was simply amused. "Ho ho ho ho ho, that. Ho ho ho ho, that is... whoo! I can't take it anymore." There were two short claps in the darkness, and then the room was flooded with light.

Dimsbury was visible as a darker area near the now blinding light being emitted from within the glass jar. After a moment, the intensity of the light faded, and it became possible to see again. Dimsbury said, "Oh, that is rich. Without a doubt, that is the finest entertainment I have seen since the comedies of the Imperial Opera. Or were they tragedies? I don't know. It's so hard to tell until the end. Do either of you sing?"

Boltac turned to face the Wizard. The light that still suffused the chamber was too powerful for anyone to notice that the lamp in his hand now glowed a little brighter than before.

Relan stumbled awkwardly into the room. Partially, it was because he had been blinded. Mostly, it was because Rattick was pushing him from behind as he held a dagger to the boy's throat.

Relan knew who it was before he heard his rasping voice.

"Undo your sword belt." commanded Rattick.

"Rattick, how could you?" asked Relan.

"Come now, boy, the question isn't how could I. The question is, how couldn't I?"

"For money, Rattick? For money, you help the man who sacked Robrecht? Your home?"

From across the room, Boltac said, "Aw c'mon kid, you didn't see that one coming? How could you not see he was working for the Wizard all along?"

"I don't work for anybody but me!" said Rattick, "But I'll take anybody's money."

Relan protested, "But we have–I mean Boltac has money. Plenty of it."

"Yes, but there is one important thing he doesn't have. A future. Dead men don't pay their bills."

"The good guys always win, Rattick. In the end, they always do," said Relan, as if it were some kind of sacred prayer.

"Only in the songs," said Rattick.

A shiver danced up Relan's spine because for the first time, the prayer wasn't enough. He didn't believe the sagas anymore. He believed the thief. Tears welled in his eyes. He wasn't the Hero he set out to be. Boltac was right. They probably weren't getting out of this alive. No one would sing songs of him. But in that darkest moment he resolved that he would meet his end like a Hero nevertheless.

Ten Orcs pushed into the room and formed a cordon around the door. Samga came with them. In comparison to these Orcs, Samga was more refined. It was as if he were a different animal altogether. Recognizable as part of the same genus, but not the same species. The ones guarding the door were more animal. They snorted and scuffled their claws against the tile. They paid careful attention to Asarah. And one of them, staring at her with unblinking, hollow, black eyes, drooled a little.

Dimsbury waved a hand, and his creatures were silenced.

"So," he said to Boltac, "What brings such an unlikely and unprepared Hero to the depths of my lair?"

"Hero?" said Boltac, trying not to let his fear show. "I ain't no Hero. You want the other guy." He jerked a thumb at Relan, who was struggling not to cut his throat by breathing too deeply against the pressure of Rattick's blade.

"Be whatever you like. The question remains, why are you here? Why are you disturbing me?"

Boltac could see no percentage in lying. He jerked his other thumb at Asarah and said, "Her."

"Oh really, is it True Love?" asked Dimsbury in a mocking tone. He rubbed his hands together with great relish. When Asarah and Boltac both blushed, he laughed. "Oh my, it *is* True Love. And I thought it was rarer than unicorns. But wait, no, it can't be True Love. Because you told me you had no interest in her. And I took you at your word as a sophisticated man of commerce."

"I said she wasn't my wife. And that doesn't give you license to steal her."

"I don't care for being stolen," said Asarah

"Yes, you are right. I have stolen her, fair and square, and she is mine. And you have come to fight for her. Fine. Take your pick of my creatures you see here before you. You may fight any one of them for her hand. Then, if you win, you may fight the rest of them. And then, if you defeat all of them, you may do battle with me."

"No," began Boltac.

"No? What do you mean no? You have come here as an *Adventurer*—as the Hero—to rescue the damsel in distress. You must fight. That's how these things are done."

"I'm not here for a fight. You stole her, fine, she's your property. But I thought perhaps we could make a deal."

"A deal? You want to BUY ME?!" protested Asarah. "Is that your idea of chivalry? Buying the woman you Love back from—"

"I never said anything about chivalry," Boltac snapped. "You know how many men have tried to defeat the great Dimsbury? You know how many have succeeded?"

"None," said Dimsbury with a great swelling of pride. "I'm entirely too powerful to be defeated by anything but a mythical Chosen One, a thing which I reasonably certain exists only within the protected confines of sagas. And if such a one does exist, I'm certain he's not a short, grubby Merchant from the backwater town of Robrecht."

"Yes, yes, mighty Dimsbury—you are wise, powerful, handsome, and tall," flattered Boltac. "A man of the world who is quick to perceive his own advantage and capitalize on it. So I offer you a lucrative trade."

Dimsbury's eyes narrowed, "A trade, you say? Tell me more."

Boltac reached into his bag and withdrew a large coin purse overflowing with gold. "I offer one hundred gold pieces for the girl."

"Girl?" Dimsbury snorted. "A handsome woman, certainly, but not a girl."

"The offer stands at one hundred," —he hefted the purse and reconsidered— "one hundred and two gold pieces for Asarah."

"But I have such a love of her mutton sandwiches. Crisp and fatty and delicious." He shivered a little to emphasize the point.

"I cannot compel one so powerful as you to do anything, but my offer presents you with a clear choice–mutton sandwiches or gold."

"Oh, that word. I cannot abide that word, OR. So harsh on the pallet, so cruel to the ear. I do not accept OR."

Boltac nodded his head deeply in recognition. "I understand Great Wizard. I understand. But all of life is a trade-off. You can't have your cake and eat it too. Surely you understand this. The money or the girl."

"No, I'll take the AND."

"The AND?" asked Boltac.

"The AND?" asked Asarah

"Hork?" grunted one of the Orcs.

"The AND," said Rattick with an approving nod. "That's what I'd take."

"Okay, so it's question of price," said Boltac.

"No, I don't think you understand," said Dimsbury with a little chuckle.

"Understand what? It's a negotiation. So, how much you want for her?"

"Boltac!" protested Asarah.

"The, uh, serving girl here," Boltac asked, giving her the signal to calm down with a downward wave of his hand behind his back. "I want my lady friend back. How much for your serving girl, my lady friend?"

"Well, *Merchant*, before we *bargain*, let me show you a few things, so that you might know what manner of man you bargain with."

"En-henh," said Boltac. Even though the Orcs did not speak English, they could hear the contempt in his voice. Several of them snarled.

Dimsbury raised his hand. "Samga, silence them or end them, I care not which."

"I hear and obey," said Samga. He whispered something in the crude, unfinished language of the Orcs. Whatever it was, the rabble blocking the door snapped to attention.

"Ah, dear Samga, with a thousand men such as you... I would still have a horde of Orcs. But a far, far better horde. At any rate, my dear Merchant, do you know what this is?" Dimsbury indicated the in-focus/out-of-focus flame that flickered on the dais next to him.

"Ehh," Boltac began, intent on making some kind of crack that would take the wind out of Dimsbury's over-stuffed sails. But the Wizard would have none of it.

"SILENCE! I will have none of your mockery and crude calculation!" With a nimbleness that Boltac would not have expected, the Wizard leapt up on the dais. He caressed the heavy glass vessel within which the flame danced. "This is beyond money. Beyond your crude buying and selling. This is the essence of the source, the headwaters of Magic itself. See how it flickers imperfectly, blurred, too pure to be fully realized on this flawed plane of existence."

Boltac rolled his eyes.

"NO!" thundered the Wizard. "This is not to be mocked. Not even slightly. This is power. POWER, do you understand? With power you can get money. But no Merchant," –he spat the title like a curse– "can ever buy power."

"Have you ever put that to the test?" Boltac asked, with a scrappiness he was faking for the purposes of negotiation. Of course, the Wizard was right, but Boltac would be damned if he'd give this twisted nobleman the satisfaction of hearing it.

To Boltac's surprise, the Wizard laughed. "Very good. Skepticism. The basis of all knowledge. Are you a seeker too, friend Boltac? Then let me show you something." Dimsbury stepped down from the dais and crossed to a small door on the far side of the room.

"Come, Merchant! I will show you what I think of money." The Wizard gestured to a spot on the wall and the blank stone changed into a doorway. "Themistres' Third Spell of Ward and Concealment. Do you know it? No matter." Dimsbury turned the knob and opened the door. "Go ahead, have a good look."

Botlac stepped forward cautiously. Overcome by curiosity and greed, Rattick moved his knife away from Relan's neck and stepped forward so he could see.

In the room beyond the door, there were chests and sacks overflowing with gold and jewels. Golden candelabras, salvers, and goblets all encrusted by the jeweler's art until it was a wonder they could still stand up under their own weight. It was the most impressive Treasure room Boltac had ever seen.

The Merchant blew a long, low whistle, "That is a lot of jingle-jangle you got there."

"So you see, your offer of gold, for the girl... here, may I?" Dimsbury reached for the purse of a hundred and two coins. Boltac handed it to him.

"Hmm, yes. Watch this." Dimsbury threw it at the feet of the Orcs. The purse broke open and gold coins scattered across the floor. Instantly the Orcs broke rank and fought for the gold pieces. Boltac jumped back. Rattick disappeared into the shadows. Only Samga remained standing, though he seemed to be under great strain.

At first it seemed like simple greed, but when an Orc got a hold of a few coins, it thrust them between its tusks and gobbled them up greedily. The pecuniary gluttony went on until there were but a few coins left. Then the Orcs began to fight over them.

"Enough!" cried Dimsbury. He clapped his hands together and there was a sound like thunder. The Orcs froze. "You see, my Orcs are hungry for gold. Not greedy, you understand, but literally *hungry* for gold. They eat it. A flaw in the design, I'm afraid: they require vast quantities of heavy minerals and metals. It's the only thing they crave more than human flesh. I am afraid I have created an armory that marches on the treasury. Upkeep is *murderous*, but then, so are they.

"So, as you see, I have quite a lot of gold, and they will mine more for supper. Your paltry hundred gold pieces are worth nothing to me, Merchant. You cannot negotiate. You have nothing I want."

"Wait, wait," Boltac said, opening his sack, "I've got more. I've got a lot of gold. I mean, I don't even know how much it is. Not as much as in your Magic room there, but it's a lot. A fortune. And this sack, it's a Magic sack. A sack of holding. Themistres'. Take it. I mean, please, you're welcome to it."

"Really," said Dimsbury. "One of old Themistres' sacks? I met him once, you know."

"Yeah, so, it's a very nice sack. This sack and all the gold in it. And, in exchange, you give me that vile-tempered woman. You don't want to own her anyway. Believe me, the upkeep on her is *real* murder."

"No one owns me," Asarah snarled.

"See what I mean?" asked Boltac, "Who needs that? I'd be doing you a favor."

"You know," Dimsbury said with a strange half-smile, "I must say, you are a civilized man."

Boltac made a little bow, "Thank you."

"Do you have any idea how many people have tried to raid my dungeon, laboratory, whatever, trying to steal my property?"

"I am not raiding you. I am a customer," he said taking pride in the title.

"Yes, here for trade. Trade is vile. But, I must admit, it is more civilized than treachery, deception, and thievery."

"Deception has its uses for the mighty," whispered Rattick from the corner of a round room. How did he do that? thought Boltac.

"Yes, civilized..." Dimsbury said, staring off into the smoky air of his spherical chamber. "I have spent so much time arguing for unreasonable people to take the civilized path."

"It's always the best way," Boltac said hopefully, "Reasonable people, getting along in a reasonable world. Able to do business together? Reasonably?" he asked hopefully.

"It is surprising," said Dimsbury.

"Funny old world, isn't it," said Boltac.

"Seize him!" commanded Dimsbury. Samga snapped his fingers and three Orcs leapt from the rabble and grabbed Boltac. Samga barked, "Take him to the cells," in the harsh tongue of the Orcs.

"No!" cried Asarah.

"Wait, wait!" cried Boltac.

"And bring the bag to me," said Dimsbury.

"Believe me, Mr. Wizard, you don't want to mess around in that bag," said Boltac as the Orcs dragged him away.

"STOP!" cried Dimsbury. "What did you say?" he asked Boltac.

"I said, for your own good, you should leave that bag alone."

"WHAT!"

"Okay, this is ridiculous. What are you, a moron? I said, stay outta the bag or you'll regret it."

"DO YOU KNOW WHO I AM?"

"Johnny Hubris?" asked Boltac. Dimsbury just stared. "He's a guy I usedta know, never mind. Look, buddy. And by 'buddy', I mean 'friend.' And by 'friend' I really mean, 'jackass.' Your hocus-pocus is gonna backfire. It always does. So how about you shut up and get on with it already."

Dimsbury clapped his hands together, and lightning bolts ricocheted around the stone chamber. Everything human in the room hid its face against the terrible noise and rush of superheated air. "I command the forces of nature. I can harness the elemental power that turns the world. And I am supposed to be afraid of your sack of goodies?"

"Only if you're not a jackass," Boltac said out of the side of his mouth.

Dimsbury crooked his fingers into a claw. Boltac was ripped from the grip of the Orcs and lifted into the air.

"Offering me a trade," Dimsbury sneered. "I have no need of your *trade*. I will take the AND. I will take your gold AND I will take your sack AND I will take your woman AND I will take your life. Did I forget anything?" He waved his other hand, and the wooden cover at the center of the chamber crashed into the ceiling and shattered into toothpicks. Dimsbury dangled Boltac over the bottomless pit.

As Dimsbury turned, he exposed his back to Relan. Strictly speaking, it wasn't the most Heroic of opportunities, but Relan seized it. His legs drove him forward. He could almost feel the Wizard's neck in his hands. He could imagine what it would feel like to bash the man's skull against the ground. He made it one step, two steps, three steps. It was going to work! He raised his hands... then felt the knife slide into his belly.

"No, no," said Rattick, still holding the lunge position that had brought him out of the shadows, "we'll have no Heroes here."

Asarah stopped sobbing and struggled to breathe.

Relan staggered forward another step, dragging Rattick with him.

Asarah pleaded with Dimsbury, "No. Don't crush him!"

"Oh, I say," Dimsbury said with a smile, "That *is* a good idea. That way it will hurt more on the way down. Goodbye, Merchant." Dimsbury opened his hand.

Boltac dropped into the bottomless pit.

34

Rattick slid the knife deeper into Relan's belly, then pulled it out. The brave Farm Boy collapsed to the floor, trying to hold his guts in.

Asarah screamed until her lungs were out of air. When she paused to take a breath, she could still hear the far off echoes of Boltac's body crashing into the sides of the pit. She screamed again, but with very little air in her lungs her cries degenerated into a cycle of shallow, choking sobs.

"Hmm, yes, thank you Rattick, for taking care of that minor nuisance."

"I live to serve, my Lord."

"It would be nice to believe that, wouldn't it, Rattick?"

"Well, whatever humble reward you see fit to bestow on my unworthy person..."

"Oh, Rattick. Oh, Faithful Rattick," he said, his voice dripping with sarcasm. "Your job was to see that no Adventurers disturbed me."

"And for that, my cut was whatever loot they had on them," Rattick said, eying Boltac's Magic sack greedily.

"Yes, but you see, I have been well and truly disturb–"

"Geh," said Relan, as the last of his life leaked out across the stone floor.

"Oh, good Lord, man, just die already and get it over with." Dimsbury looked at Asarah, collapsed in a heap on the ground. "You'll clean this up! I swear to the Nether Gods you will. They're *your* rescuers. This is *your* mess. Now, where was I? Oh yes, Rattick. I know not what to do with you."

"I just saved your life, Master."

"You saved my robe, Rattick. You think he had a chance?"

"Eeeh..." said Rattick.

Dimsbury bent over and addressed the dying boy directly, "You never had a chance! Do you understand? Not a chance."

Relan made a gurgling noise.

"So, Rattick, I will allow you to take as much gold as you can gather and carry from Boltac's sack. Is that acceptable?"

"Quite acceptable."

"Excellent. And I trust I will never see you again."

"Not in this or any other lifetime," Rattick said, with a courtly bow of his head.

"Very well. Samga, take the sack to the UnderHall, gather the horde, and dump the Merchant's gold for the feast."

"As you command, Master."

"But," Rattick interrupted, as gently as possible, "I take mine first, right?"

"Oh, no Rattick. Where is the sport in that? No, you can scrabble and claw for your reward with the rest of my creatures. Conduct him to the UnderHall and give him the place of honor," Dimsbury said with a smile. Rattick was quickly surrounded by Orcs and led from the room.

As he left, he had just enough time to say, "You are too kind, Master."

Dimsbury dismissed him with an annoyed wave.

"What shall I do about this one, Lord?" asked Samga, nodding at Relan.

"Leave him to die slowly. Kill him not. But when he is done, you may feed him to whatever Orcs you deem worthy of reward. Or keep him for yourself, Samga. You deserve it for keeping this rabble in line."

"They will be so pleased, Master," said Samga.

"I am a good and gentle Master, am I not?"

"The finest Master," said Samga.

"Now I am off to my chambers. I simply must rest. And the first creature to disturb me will not remain a creature. Am I understood?"

Samga nodded. Dimsbury left. Samga remained for a moment, considering the horrible scene before him. Beneath Asarah's choking sobs, could hear the labored, gurgling breathing of the dying lad. He twitched his head once, then hurried off to his duties.

35

Boltac awoke to more pain than he'd realized the world could hold. It was a universe of pain, a cosmos of pain, and he was at the center of it. In the darkness there was only pain. He tried to open his eyes and there was pain. He tried to close his half-opened eyes and there was pain. His body made the mistake of trying to cough. Then the darkness took him again. He didn't even have time to ask how it might be that he was still alive.

An age, a time, or a moment later, he awoke again. There was a soft rustling in the darkness beside him, and he felt the touch of many creatures he could not see. It was not comforting.

"Wha–" he tried to ask, but too many ribs were broken for him to speak. He wheezed in pain. The soft touches–were they hands, or something else?–migrated to his side. Under their strange caresses, the pain eased. As he controlled his loud and labored breathing, he became aware of a low, whispered song all around him. It disappeared into the blackness with no echo, as if he were in a room so vast as to have no walls.

After a time, the pain in his side was soothed. His breathing came more easily. Unexpectedly, his body was wracked with sobs. In that place of dry darkness, tears streamed down his face and some infinite softness blotted them away. "I should be dead," Boltac said at last.

"Someday, you will be," said the voice in the darkness.

"Is this Magic?"

"Magic? We are merely flawed creatures caring for one of our kind. But there is a Magic in that, yes."

The voice said nothing else. The silence made Boltac nervous, so he joked, "I guess this bottomless pit had a bottom after all."

"There is no such thing as a bottomless pit," said the voice in the darkness.

"No such thing as a free lunch either," said Boltac. "So, who are you and why are you helping me?"

"We are the fallen ones, the discarded ones. The ones that were made, but not unmade."

"En-henh," Boltac said, trying to sit up and immediately regretting it.

"Be still. Your kind was also made, once. And you, as broken as you are, are not beyond salvation, if you will allow it."

"Ho-oh boy. What is going on here? Am I dead? Did I have to pay for own my funeral?"

"We have been shaped and have learned something of the shaping of life. We are the forgotten ones. The made and discarded."

"Wait, wait, you are..."

"The Wizard's forgotten sons. The ones he made and thought to unmake by discarding us in this place."

"So, uh, forgive me if this is a rude question, but why aren't ya dead? For that matter, how come I'm still here?"

"When he made us, he did not weave a full spell. He did not allow for the possibility of death. So we must go on for eternity."

"Wait? You mean you can't die?"

"A horse can die, for it is alive. But we are like the carriage. We are not alive, but we function. We cannot die. Only fall apart for all eternity. Unless..."

The singing stopped.

"Unless what? What's the catch? There's always a catch," said Boltac.

"We have done all we can for you."

"And thanks for that. I don't feel good, but I don't feel dead either."

"No life should be discarded."

"You don't get around much do you?" Boltac asked the voice. "Who are you? Not the plural you, not youse, but you in particular."

"I am the UnderKing, First among the Broken."

"Oh, sorry about that, your honor, my liege, whatever. I didn't realize your kind had nobles."

"We did not. But in the darkness, nobility is called forth by need."

"En-henh? Come again?"

The UnderKing paused for a long time before continuing. "The Flame, the one the Wizard worships."

"You mean the 'Source of All Magic'?"

"The very one. We do not know how he came to hold it. We only know that it makes him powerful beyond all those who have come before him. When once his Magic is depleted, one touch of the Flame restores him."

"But there's a catch," said Boltac, "There's always a catch. No such thing as a free bottomless pit."

"The Wizard's Magic–ALL Magic–draws from the source. If the Flame of Magic is extinguished, Magic and everything that it has wrought will end... and we will be released."

"So, ya telling me there's a way to snuff out Magic? Like a candle?"

"Yes," said the UnderKing, "but only a Hero, a true Hero, one Chosen by fate and circumstance can overcome the Wizard and quench the torrent of Magic. That is why you–"

"Wait a minute. Wait a minute! You're saying I'm the Chosen One? Like *Chosen*? Look buddy, no offense, but I'm just a guy trying to make a coin in this world, you understand?"

"In your heart, there is Love."

"Yeah. Love of coin."

"There is more," said the UnderKing. "Do not lie to me. Do not lie in this place, of all places. There is no bargain you can make with the final darkness."

"There's always room to negotiate."

"Not at the very end."

"C'mon, all the stories and the sagas and the miracle turnarounds...?"

Silence.

"Look, I'm not your guy. I'm sorry. The guy you wanted, your *Hero*, is lying up there in a pool of his own blood and entrails. He was an idiot, but he was the better man. No thought for himself at all. What a jackass! I wish I could be like him, but I'm not. I'm not your Hero, so..."

"What of the girl?" the UnderKing asked.

"What, Asarah? Okay, look, I love her. I do. And I figured it out too late. I blew it. So now I'm here, where ever the hell *here* is. I got the kid killed and there's nuttin' I can do about any of it. It sucks, but that's business. I can't save her. I... can't..."

Wise in the ways of patience, the UnderKing said nothing.

"I can't even save myself. I thought I was a smart guy. I thought I had a clever plan, but now... none of my plans are clever. I'm just a fool. So, you know, kill me or whatever you're going to do."

"You are a broken thing," said the UnderKing.

"Yeah. Broken. No resale value whatsoever. So what do I do now?"

"When in darkness, follow the light," said the UnderKing as his voice retreated from Boltac.

"What? There's no light down here. It's the bottom of a bottomless pit!"

36

Boltac sat in the dark for a long time. There are many more gradations of darkness than the human eye can see. In fact, it is correct to say that humans cannot see any kind of darkness at all, only light. But there is always a catch. As Boltac stared into that endless night and saw nothing, he realized there was a patch of blackness that he couldn't see, but it was a patch of blackness that he couldn't see a little less than all the other blackness surrounding it.

Very slowly, and with many groans, he got to his feet. His clothes, what were left of them, were in tatters. But when he felt his limbs and torso, he realized that, somehow, he had been made whole. His ribs had stopped moving under his skin like a sack of broken sticks. The strange pads and paws of the Broken Ones had somehow set him to rights. For a moment, he considered that he might be a thing made, just as they were.

"You are a broken thing." The UnderKing's words echoed in his ears. In the vast silence surrounding him, the imagined voice was deafening.

Boltac took a step towards the less-dark darkness. It was unnerving to walk blindly. He slid his foot across the floor, expecting a pit, or a knife in his back, or any one of a thousand injuries or tortures or traps that his mind conjured in the absence of anything to look at.

Even moving at a snail's pace, Boltac broke out a cold sweat. But inch by inch, he moved forward. After a time he could not measure, he realized that the unseeable floor beneath his feet was sloping upward. But to where? How far had he fallen? There might have been no such thing as a bottomless pit, but there were surely deep, deep holes in the earth.

He came to a wall and felt his way along it in the dark. His hands clung to every fissure and rough place with greed and desperation, as if he could fall off into the darkness and be lost forever. As he walked, he was overcome with the hopelessness of his position. He was miles underground and could wander forever–or at least until dehydration killed him–without ever finding his way out.

"Follow the light?" Boltac called out. "Hey! I'm talking to you. I know there's something out there... in here... whatever..." he said, assured at first, but his voice trailing off at the end. He thought for a while about all the somethings that could be out there in the darkness. Maybe yelling was a bad idea. Maybe breathing was a bad idea. Maybe everything was a bad idea.

Boltac laid his head against the wall and fought back tears. As silent sobs wracked his body, his necklace of charms made infinitesimal jingling noises against the stone. Did he have a ward against being trapped underground? He'd have to get one of those. When he got out of here that would be the first thing he would do. Surely those barbarous, tanned Southroners had a God of the UnderDark or some such. Who did the UnderKing worship, Boltac wondered? Somewhere, *somebody* had to have a charm against this kind of thing, and Boltac would find it.

Wiping his tears away with what remained of his sleeve, Boltac pressed on. A few steps later, he found an opening in the wall and in it, stairs. As he climbed, he realized that the steps were cut for a creature with a smaller stride than a human. It made climbing them even harder than climbing regular stairs. But even though his legs cramped and his lungs burned, he climbed. Not quickly. Not as a young man like Relan might, but slowly and without stopping.

• • •

When the sound of Boltac's footsteps rising from the UnderDark had faded, Samga spoke to the UnderKing. "I told you he was not the one."

"It is not done yet," said the UnderKing.

"He's no Chosen One. He cannot release us from The Master."

"Maybe it is not the one who is Chosen who can save us, Samga. Maybe it is the one who *chooses*."

"I have been away too long," said Samga, turning to leave his King.

"I will await his return for a time."

"Of course," said Samga, "All you ever do is sit in the dark and wait."

Samga followed his own scent-trail back to the secret fissure he would climb back to the Wizard's dungeon. He had thought he was out range of the UnderKing, but all of a sudden his voice was there beside him.

"It is not all sitting and waiting, Samga. The darkness is where an Orc can look inward; here, there is nothing else to see."

"We were made hollow. We are empty inside."

"It is not done yet," said the UnderKing, knowing that those words were always true.

37

Boltac stumbled through darkness for what felt like days. The stairs ended in another darkened level. Again, he felt his way towards the lighter darkness. He stumbled into walls. Once he almost fell into a pit. His nerves became numb to the constant strain, even as his hands cramped with the effort of extending outward as far as his fingers could reach. Eventually, the ache reached all the way to his shoulders.

He was on the verge of giving up, when he felt a faint stirring of air. It was not the stale reek of the depths. It was light and sweet, like a cool drink of water on a hot summer day. His lungs drank it in greedily, and he followed the scent and movement of that impossible breeze.

He rounded a corner and then he saw it. Light. Not the brightness of a new day dawning. Not even the faint light of a candle guttering its last spark in a pool of melted tallow. It was, perhaps, the faintest light a man can see. But compared to the void from which he had come it was a beacon to light his way. He hurried and fell. Got up and fell again. Climbed stairs using his hands and feet. Then a passage to the left, more stairs and there it was: a chink in the wall. A pure beam of sunlight in this darkened place.

He followed the beam to its source, a hole in an ancient stone door choked with vines on the other side. After a struggle with the stone, he was able to pull it open. Grass, vines, and sod fell in as he pushed his way out into the sunlight and open air.

He saw that he was high on the side of a mountain, facing east; the light was the sun shining through the forest canopy. Near him, a spring burbled down the slope. Boltac drank greedily from it. It was so clear and cold it made his teeth ache. When he splashed it upon his shaven pate, the shock of it sparked through him an emotion that was very much like hope. Realizing he was alive, free, and in the light of a new day, Boltac laughed as he had not laughed for years.

A short walk in the sunlight, a gentle stroll downhill and around the base of this mountain would put him on the road back home. He had it on good authority that some people even enjoyed such walks in the woods.

And then what? Sell what was left in his store. Buy a boat and head south? A leisurely drift down the river Swift. Some fishing along the way. Bonfires on the riverbank at night.

And then what? A shop or trading stall in Yorn or in the swamp-ringed Squalipoor? Surely he would not stop in Shatnapur? That would be too close to Robrecht. Too close to memories. Too close to...

And then what? Build a business again. Make back something of the fortune he'd lost. He could do it. Wasn't he a lucky man? As he thought this, he jangled the necklace of charms and wards. A lucky man. Luck earned with hard work and the money it had brought.

And then what? His ease in old age, perhaps a place to put his feet up? He wasn't too old to dream of a family. A vineyard, something productive, not too far out of a city, but away from the bustle. And then, as an old man, the busy-ness of his life complete, he would put his feet on the hearth, sip the wine that was too good to sell, and he would have time to think.

To think of what? Boltac looked back toward the stone door through which he'd escaped. To think of Relan falling to the stone floor. The look of confusion on his face that said, "But this can't happen. I am the Hero!" To think of Asarah, lost to him. As lost to him as if she were dead. But her scream, her wails, crying for him. Would he not hear that screaming echo for the rest of his life?

He turned away from the door. "No. It was a bad deal from the beginning, but you got away with your skin. It's a sunk cost, Boltac. Take the hit and walk away." He nodded to himself as if that ended the argument. Good. Sensible. Mercantile. Just a bad deal. But when he went to walk away, his feet moved in the wrong direction, back toward the door, toward Asarah and Relan, Glory and Treasure, Wizard and Orcs...

He stopped himself. "Who am I kidding?" he asked the bright new day. "I'm just gonna get myself killed. I'm not the Chosen One. Who chose me? Who ever *would* choose me? I'm not a Hero. I don't have broad shoulders or Shining™ Armor. I'm not even young anymore."

He fingered the necklace thick with charms and got an idea. It was a bad idea. But then, this whole thing had been a bad idea from the get-go. Boltac made his decision. He drew himself up and squared his shoulders. "You make your own luck," he said to no one, hoping he sounded more certain than he felt.

He took a deep breath of fresh air. He said goodbye to the trees and the green grass and the water pure and dancing through the rocks. The clouds parted and the sun was too bright. He squinted and bade a silent last goodbye to the world. Then he headed back into the darkness. It was a bad deal all right, thought Boltac. But he had made it, and he wasn't going to break it.

Was he putting his life at risk? Sure, thought Boltac. But that was nothing. It wasn't just the sum of all his yesterdays he had put up to finance this ill-advised expedition. It was the promise of all his tomorrows. Unless he saw this thing through, there would be no ease by the fire. There would be no pleasure in shrewd trading and crisp profits. There would be no living with himself.

And Asarah? thought Boltac. She Loves me not. But I Love her still, Gods help me; I can do nothing else. A thought surfaced in his mind: I guess that makes me some kind of Hero. As he closed the door behind him, he answered his mind's foolishness with a skeptical, "En-henh."

It was harder to go back. Now he could appreciate how stagnant the air really was down here. Each step still brought fear, but they were now robbed of hope and anticipation: he knew what awaited him at the bottom of the pit. So he followed the dark, sinking in the blackness, this time following his own compass of stale fear and dry death.

When at last he came to the gigantic, silent room, he stood listening for a time. He heard nothing, but took a chance anyway. "I know you're there," he said.

"You have returned," said the UnderKing. "Why?"

"I need to find a way up."

"We told you, to find your way out, you must follow the light."

"Not *out*, back up. Into the mess. And with all the crap the Wizard has thrown down this hidey hole, you can't tell me there's not a friggin' torch down here somewhere."

"But this is the UnderDark," said the UnderKing. "The Kingdom of Things Discarded that Wish to be Forgotten–"

"Yeah, yeah, that's one hell of pitch for tourism, but if you want to me to take on this crazy Wizard at the height of his power, I gotta get up there first. For that I need light."

In the darkness, a light appeared. It was a torch, and though it was soaked in oil and burning well, the darkness did not give up easily. It pressed in on all sides. As the torch was lifted, Boltac saw that it was Samga who held it. To his left, wearing a crown of bent and twisted metal, stood a simpler, cruder version of an Orc. The UnderKing closed his eyes and shielded them from the light with his claw. His features seemed drawn in crayon, simple and plain. A moon face, mere holes for ears, and a scribble for a mouth. His simple symmetry was interrupted by a leg bent underneath him, twisted as if it had shattered in a fall and never properly reset.

"Uh," began Boltac, then realized that the emptiness of the pit was anything but empty.

At the very edges of the feeble light cast by the torch were creatures keeping to the dark. Some walked, some crawled, some shambled, all moved silently and whispered in unison: "Release. Release. Release."

Boltac tore his eyes away from the shapes in the darkness and looked at Samga. "Why are you helping me? Why do you betray your Master?"

"Do you have a Master?"

"No."

"Do you want one?"

"No."

"Neither do I. This is my King," Samga nodded towards the Under-King. Then he looked up and said, "He is my captor."

"Okay, well. Good enough for me. Now, let's talk about how we are going to do this. We need to be patient. Take our time. Make no mistakes. We're only gonna get one shot at this guy."

Samga's expression did not change when he said, "He has bled the boy dry to lure the Flame, and soon will sacrifice the woman. By so doing, he shall weld the Flame to his power."

"What?"

"It is blood Magic. The force that binds mother to child, father to son, and clan to clan. Very old and very powerful," said Samga.

"You forgot *very* crazy," said Boltac.

"He hungers for power and cares not how he gets it."

"En-henh. Okay, no offense to your hospitality here, King, but we need to get a move on. I'm late for an appointment to do something stupid."

Not opening his eyes, the UnderKing said, "Blessings be upon you, One who has Chosen."

"En-henh. I see what you did there."

As Samga walked away, the broken ones skittered out of the range of light. Boltac followed. He didn't feel lucky, but at least he didn't feel broken anymore.

38

When the Wizard returned to his sanctum, Asarah crept as far under the table as her chain would allow. She sat wide-eyed and frozen like a rabbit who hopes the fox does not see her.

But at that moment, Dimsbury had no attention to spare for her. As soon as he entered the room he was drawn to the Flame. He muttered to himself, "Brighter. More resolved. But how can this be?" Dimsbury looked around the chamber. He waved a hand at the wall sconces, and they burst into flame, overpowering the uncertain Magic Flame and filling the room with an honest, if sooty, light.

A glance down revealed the cause. From Relan's body, a rivulet of blood flowed across the floor to the dais on which the Flame sat. "Could it be?" Dimsbury asked. He bent, dipped his fingers into the blood, and held them above the Flame. As blood dripped downward into the confluence of Magic, the Flame was transformed through a brilliant range of hues, and seemed more substantial at the end of it.

Dimsbury turned to what was left of Relan and said, "You're not completely useless after all, what a pleasant surprise!"

The Wizard wasted no time in having Relan strung up by his ankles over the Flame. What little blood remained in the poor boy dripped into the cool, hypnotic light. The Flame lapped greedily at the blood and became more focused and defined with each drop.

Asarah wept at the gruesome sight. She wept for Relan, who had tried to be a Hero and had failed. And now the stuff of his life was drained out to... it was horrible. She wept for herself, surely about to meet the same end. And yes, she wept for Boltac. He was no Hero. He was not equipped even to save himself. But still, he had come for her.

She had forgotten her earlier words, but now they came back: "But that's how she *knows* that he truly Loves her." Boltac wasn't a prince. This wasn't a storybook or a saga, but he had come for her. It was not what she expected from romance, but it was true. Or had been. Now Boltac was dead, never to return. And she had been so cruel to him.

Grief piled upon grief and sorrow upon sorrow. But she was so afraid, she dared not give voice to her pain. Silent tears streamed down her face as if they could flood the interior of the earth.

When Relan's blood stopped flowing, Dimsbury swung him away from the Flame and hacked the cords holding him up with a knife. The lad's body fell to the floor in an awful heap.

Without looking at Asarah, Dimsbury addressed her in a voice loud enough to make her jump. "My dear, I have good news and bad news!"

She did not answer. She did not even move.

"The good news is that I no longer require you to be my cook."

All thought left Asarah. She screamed.

"Seize her!" Dimsbury commanded. The screaming was perfect, thought Dimsbury. It was all according to form, the way such things were to be done. But the Orcs did not move towards her. This wasn't right at all. It made her scream seem pointless and silly.

Exasperated, Dimsbury exclaimed, "Her, there under the table. Grab her. Her. THAT ONE!" He made wild, uninterpretable thrashing gestures with his hands. "The screaming one!"

The Orcs finally got the idea and seized the woman. As they dragged her out, she struggled so violently that she knocked herself unconscious on the table leg. As Dimsbury watched the Orcs tie her feet to the ropes that would dangle her above the Flame of Magic, he wondered aloud, "Where is Samga? He was here just a minute ago."

39

Rattick had not pushed his luck. After killing the boy, he had left the Wizard's presence as quickly as possible. Sure, there was the question of payment owed, but Rattick knew as well as anyone that dead men collect no tolls or tithes. Best to stay alive, for there was no profit in death. The Orcs carried Boltac's sack high above their heads, fighting over it as they raced to the Great Hall. Rattick followed in the shadows, waiting for his chance to grab something of value before he escaped from the madness of the Wizard's lair. Why were rich people always so dangerously out of touch with reality? Rattick wondered.

The Great Hall was ambitiously named yet modestly furnished. A large cavern off the main passage, it was a darker analog of a refectory at a traditional boy's school. Large wooden tables with benches had once been lined up here. Now half of them were pushed into a jumble at the far end of the room. A mock fireplace carved into the living rock was full to overflowing with bits of discarded bone and gristle. Here and there, a wolf nosed through the scraps. Even to Rattick, this jumbled room looked like the end of a civilization.

Concealed by his cloak, he climbed the rough chamber wall and shimmied down a thick iron chain to a long unused chandelier. There he took up his perch and watched and waited.

The Orcs cleared a space in the center of the room where they fought over the bag. Claws darted in here and there, trying to snatch the contents. The room quickly filled to capacity with the brutish creatures. The noise of their disputations was deafening. The smell of so many of them, packed so close was debilitating. Rattick began to wonder if the chandelier had been a terrible idea. But he remained still and silent. There was nothing else to do.

Soon the bag was upended, and the contents spilled all over the floor. For such a tiny, plain bag, it was shocking to see how much it contained. Among the miscellany–the occasional weapon, rations of food, bits of apparel–came sack after sack of coin. They poured from the opening, landing on the floor with solid, seductive clinks of loot. What would they do with the gold? Rattick wondered. He decided to wait until they were tired of fighting amongst themselves. Then he would swoop down and collect as many of those sacks as he could.

Rattick's dreams of avarice were shattered as he watched Orcs claw the leather bags apart and cram the gold pieces in their mouths. They clawed and fought and ate until all of Boltac's gold– of which there was a substantial fortune–had disappeared into their monstrous gullets. Rattick sighed and felt an emotion that was very much like grief. Ah well, the dungeon had been good while it lasted, he thought. He'd wait for the creatures to disband then he would sneak out like the thief he was.

But the Orcs did not leave. Their squabbles gradually died down until, bloated on coin, they fell asleep under, on, and around the tables. Rattick cursed his luck and shifted his cramping legs. How much longer would he be stuck up here? He waited until the strange snores of the Orcs below wafted up to his ears. Then he uncoiled himself from his perch and climbed back down.

He snuck through the sated and sedate creatures as quietly as he could. When one near the door snorted heavily and rolled over, Rattick swore he could hear coins rattling in his belly. A plan suggested itself to Rattick. And, with Rattick, where there was a plan, there was almost always a sharp knife involved. He drew his cruel blade from the sheath on his thigh and considered how he might do this quietly. With an ordinary person, he would just cram a hand over the mouth and slide the dagger down into the neck. This would sever an artery deep inside the torso so that the person would bleed to death internally in a matter of seconds. It was very clean and very professional. Rattick prided himself on his knowledge of this assassin's technique.

But with an Orc, this presented a number of problems. Not least of which: how do you cover a mouth that has tusks? And he had seen how brutishly powerful these things were. He doubted that they would die quietly. How could he hope to hold this one down? He hunkered in a nearby shadow and considered his prey. As he did, out of habit, he drew a whetstone from a pouch on his belt, spit on it, and began to sharpen the already razor-sharp knife. There was gold enough here. He just needed to figure out how to cut off a piece for himself.

When he heard a noise from outside, he replaced the knife and sharpening stone and then hid his hands under his robe. As the clawsteps drew closer, he closed his eyes so that the whites of them might not give him away when whoever it was entered. This was an old and important trick of Rattick's. Hiding was a fine art, relying as much upon psychology as camouflage. The only time people looked carefully at a room was when they first walked in. Once they believed they knew who and what was there, it became very difficult for them to see anything new. It wasn't so much hiding in plain sight as hiding in someone else's self-enforced blind spot.

He heard another Orc enter the room. There was a shuffling and a scraping of claws. But there was no sharp intake of breath. No sudden movements. Rattick remained unseen. Then the Orc spoke, but in the human tongue.

"It is safe, they are all asleep," said a voice both alien and familiar to Rattick. He opened his eyes and saw Samga, the Wizard's clever Orc. And entering the room behind him... BOLTAC! In spite of his own general and considerable sneakitude, Rattick jumped at the sight of Boltac and struggled to stifle a curse.

"Well, somebody had a party," said Boltac. "Did they eat everything?"

"Most likely just the metals."

"Good, 'cause there's a couple of things it would be nice to have," Boltac said as he searched the wreckage of the room. After a few moments, he held up a half-chewed, heavy wool mitten. "I suppose the other one is too much to ask for. See if you can find a wand, or the sack."

Samga held up a shredded mass of fabric that had once been a Magic sack. "You mean this?"

"Ah, crap," said Boltac. He took the burlap from Samga and examined it carefully. The torn shred contained nothing. Boltac turned it over and then over again. As he folded and unfolded it, something fell out onto the floor. It was a small, lacquered box. "Enh. Well, it's better than nuttin'," said Boltac as he tucked the box inside his tunic. "Well, if that's all we got, it looks like we'll be doing this the hard way, unless..." Boltac looked around the room at the sleeping Orcs and their bloated bellies. "You know, Samga, there was a lot of gold in that sack of mine. An awful lot. Did they eat all of it?"

"They kept eating until there was nothing left to eat," Samga said with a shrug.

"En-henh. Not sophisticated and restrained like you."

"As you say," Samga said, surveying his kin with sadness. "All of your gold is gone. Such a shame."

"It's not gone," said Boltac, "It's in your friends' stomachs, here. Important distinction."

Samga did not understand much of anything humans said. The gold was eaten. And that other word, he had never heard it before, "Please, what does this word 'friend' mean."

"Ya kiddin' me, right?" said Boltac.

Samga gave him a flat Orc-ish look that admitted of no humor.

"Okay. You, Samga, you're my *friend*. You are *helping* me, ergo, you are my friend," said Boltac.

"But I am just hurting The Master," said Samga.

"Yeah, it's a trade. You help me by getting me out. I help you by hurting The Master, and we both benefit. Trade makes friends, Samga."

"But you cannot be friends with such as I. I am beneath you."

"What? Don't be ridiculous. Beneath me? I mean, ya short, there's no way around that. But I know good people. You, Samga, you are good people. Uh, Orcle? Whatever, c'mon. I still got a lady to rescue."

Then Boltac noticed his Magic-detecting wand, trapped under a sleeping Orc's leg. "Hey, uh, Samga, could you..." He pointed at the wand. "Probably better you than me if this thing wakes up."

Samga lifted the leg and retrieved the Magic-detecting wand. It, too, had been gnawed on but had fared better than the bag and mittens. Boltac used what remained of his tunic to wipe the saliva from it.

"Okay, this will do, now let's get outta here." They returned to the door. Rattick thought that Boltac looked right through him–right into his eyes–but Boltac's eye was drawn to something on the right side of the door.

"Hey," Boltac said, "The sacred Lantern of Lamptopolis."

"Lamptopolis?" asked Samga.

"Eh, never mind. It's a long story. The damn thing doesn't really work that well for me, but, as I always say, you can never have too much light or too much water." Boltac reached down and grabbed the lamp by its handle. As he held it up, it blazed forth with a clear, brilliant light that filled the room as if the sun had been harnessed and dragged into the bowels of the earth.

Samga hissed and averted his eyes. Rattick covered his eyes to protect his night vision, but otherwise stayed absolutely motionless. For an instant, he was completely exposed, but there was nothing to be done.

"Holy crap!" Boltac said, and dropped the lamp with a clatter. Its light gradually faded away. Rubbing residual spots of brilliance from his eyes, Boltac stood over the lamp, confused. "I don't understand. I mean, I'm not–"

"We must go!" said Samga.

Boltac looked up and realized that the Orcs, awakened by the commotion, had begun to stir. He grabbed the remnants of Themistre's Bag of Holding and wrapped them around the lamp handle. This time, when he picked up the lamp, it did not light. He flipped a loose end of the burlap over the lamp's motto. "Burns with the Flame of a True Heart," Boltac muttered. "En-henh."

One of the lethargic Orcs saw them go. The creature cried, "Hork!" but it was a half-hearted protest at best. The gold, heavy in its belly, made it difficult to rise.

Rattick slipped out of the shadows. How had Boltac survived his fall into the bottomless pit? And where was he headed now? Rattick sensed chaos. And where chaos rode, there were always plenty of spoils for the taking. He followed the Merchant and his unlikely guide.

40

"Samga. There you are," said Dimsbury. He stood on the dais next to the Magic Flame. Above the dais Asarah hung by her legs. "Thank the Gods you have returned. Pass me that knife over there so I may open this woman's neck." Asarah attempted a scream, but it was muffled by a gag, which Dimsbury now tightened. "I must say, woman, I enjoy your company much more now that you are quiet. I will almost be sad to see you go. Samga, the knife!"

From over his shoulder, Dimsbury heard Samga say, "No."

"'No'? What do you mean 'no'? There is no 'no'!"

The Wizard turned to see a smiling Boltac standing next to his prized creature. "Samga, what do you have there? And wherever did you find it?"

"Back like a bad penny," said Boltac.

"Before we get to the question of *how,*" Dimsbury said wearily, "I must ask you: why?"

"I'm here to do you in."

Dimsbury gestured, vaguely, at Relan's body, now discarded along the wall. "Yes, that was his idea as well. What makes you think you will fare any better?"

"I am not an idiot."

"Idiots are always the last to find out," said Dimsbury

"Eh-henh. You want I should say touché or something, or can we just get down to business?"

"Very well," said Dimsbury, and picked up a medium-sized silver whistle from his desk. "I shall let my staff handle the light work."

He placed his lips to the whistle and blew. No sound came from the whistle, but Samga writhed in pain.

From outside there was a groaning commotion. Soon, metal-bloated Orcs streamed into the room. They snorted and growled and clanked and bitched in their brutish language about being awakened from their post-gluttony slumber. And, if such a thing were possible, they seemed even more frightening and contentious than Orcs usually did.

Dimsbury drew himself up to his full height. He lifted his arms and electricity crackled along his fingertips and the surface of his robes. In full voice, he began his mighty, doom-filled pronouncement. "Tear him—"

"Hang on," said Boltac, "Hang on. Sorry to ruin your speech there. But I've got one of those too." Boltac reached for his charm necklace. For the first time in a long time, he felt very, very lucky. He placed the tiny silver whistle to his lips and blew.

Nothing happened.

"I'm sorry, is that it?" asked Dimsbury, his voice dripping with contempt.

"Eh, hang on," Boltac put the whistle to his lips again and blew as hard as he could. Blew until he was red in the face. Blew until he was sputtering and out of air. He finished with a defeated "huuuuuuuuh" as and then he gasped for air.

The Orcs looked at Boltac. Samga looked at Boltac. Hanging upside down, Asarah closed her eyes.

"Yes," said Dimsbury, "if you are quite through?" Boltac looked down and away. "TEAR HIM LIMB FROM LIMB!"

There was nowhere to run. There was nothing to do. As the first Orc advanced, Boltac turned to Samga, "Sorry. I thought that would work."

Snarling, the front line of Orcs reached for Boltac. Their claws and tusks searched in savage arcs for the soft, fat flesh of the Merchant. But before Boltac was torn open, the biggest Orc of all let out a long howl of pain. The other Orcs stopped to watch as it grasped its stomach and collapsed to the floor. Then another fell, and then another, until all of them were lying on the floor, writhing in pain.

"What is this foolishness?" demanded Dimsbury.

Boltac resumed blowing his whistle for all he was worth. As the Orcs writhed in agony on the floor, the largest of them made the connection. He lifted his taloned hand off the ground then plunged it deeply into his own stomach. The whistle dropped from Boltac's lips has his face contorted in disgust. Coins exploded outward from the unfortunate creature's stomach. Some spewed to the ground with gouts of blood and intestine. Others clicked and clinked as they ripped tiny slices of flesh from the now dying creature.

Boltac pumped one fist in victory. "NO SUCH THING AS A FREE LUNCH!" he shouted. The Creeping Coins crawled and swarmed over the Orcs, tearing them apart with the gnashing of thousands of tiny teeth.

A bolt of lightning exploded across the room.

Boltac held up his hand with the one Gauntlet of Magic Negation. It absorbed Dimsbury's lightning bolt. "Hey! That worked!" Boltac said, laughing giddily.

Dimsbury furrowed his brow and said, "Very well. The fat man wants to play."

The next bolt of lightning was so powerful Boltac thought his eyeballs had been seared from his head. When his sight returned from momentary blindness, he saw that the mitten on his left hand remained intact. As Dimsbury extended his arm again, Boltac closed his eyes. He felt an impact, and another, and another. The palm of the mitten grew hot and he fought off the urge to shake his hand. On his belt, the Magic-detecting wand vibrated wildly. "Okay," said Boltac, "this isn't funny anymore."

"Do something!" Samga cried over the crackle of the lightning and the rush of superheated air.

"I can't see!" protested Boltac. And the bolts kept coming and coming, pounding into his left arm. He could feel the mitten burning his flesh. And now tiny shocks, the leftover current that the Gauntlet could not absorb, forced the muscles of his arm to contract and twitch violently. He turned his face away from the Wizard, still holding his hand up. Eyes closed in a painful wince, he felt around for something, anything...

Samga pushed the heavy shelves over. They toppled into Dimsbury and knocked him back a step. The Wizard lashed out blindly, and a bolt of electricity caught Samga in the chest. Samga staggered backward, then collapsed. As Dimsbury turned back, he saw Boltac throw his wand across the room.

"Ha!" cried Boltac as the wand spun through the air. Dimsbury sneered and raised his hand to launch another blast at the now-distracted Merchant. But as the wand flew toward Dimsbury, it suddenly veered off toward the jar on the dais, drawn inexorably to the Flame.

Boltac gaped. He'd seen the wand react in any number of disturbing ways to potent Magic. What it would do in the presence of its very source, he had no idea.

The wand dived into the jar, there was a wuffing sound, and the Flame snapped into sharp focus. The wand reached the heart of the Flame and stopped moving. Everything stopped moving.

Boltac ran to the dais, swung Asarah off to the side and her to the ground. As he knelt to untie her, he felt rather than heard the high-pitched whine growing louder and louder, and a buzzing and clacking that raised the hair on the back of his neck. Looking up at the dais, he saw the Magic-detecting wand flying and whirling in the Flame, its brass tip chipping away at the inside of the jar.

"What have you done?" Dimsbury screamed. Then he realized he didn't care. He threw his hands forward in a gesture of power that was certain to obliterate Boltac. But nothing happened.

Dimsbury looked at his hands, confused, and tried again. "STOP!" he commanded. Still, nothing happened. "What have you done?" he asked weakly.

Dimsbury turned toward the dais and the brilliant Flame trapped by the frenzied wand. The flow of Magic, yes, he thought, that's what it had to be. The flow of Magic had been blocked. The pressure was building up behind it. Inside the illuminated jar the wand spun furiously, emitting the high-pitched, rising whine that dominated the room. If Dimsbury could stop the wand, unblock the flow. He reached out, trembling, and touched one fingertip to the protective jar.

Boltac threw himself over Asarah. "Stay down," he shouted in her ear.

As Dimsbury's finger brushed the surface of the jar, the glass shattered into a million fragments, each of those fragments shattering again with the force of the exploding Flame.

The explosion knocked everyone flat. So close to the dais, Boltac was spared the worst of the blast, Asarah safe beneath him. Samga, still surprised to have survived a bolt of lightning to his chest, had just risen to his hands and knees. He saw Dimsbury fly over his head, then the blast threw him across the room. He landed next to what was left of Relan. Even the Creeping Coins were flung about so violently they retracted into their glittering carapaces and pretended to be currency.

As Boltac raised his head, he heard a moan coming from Relan's corpse. Wait! Moan? Not a corpse! Somehow Relan was still alive!?! "Too stupid to die?" Boltac asked. Then he searched in his tunic for the small lacquered box. His hands shook as he opened it. Within lay a tiny flask covered in ornately wrapped gold wire. No bigger than Boltac's thumb, this vial looked as if it could contain no more than the amount of liquid found in a few tears.

Boltac looked at the heap of Relan. The blood soaked into his tunic was already turning brown. There was no color left in his face. The boy's lips were blue, but still his chest rose and fell. How was it that he lived? Was this not another kind of Magic? The Magic of will alone?

"Kid," Boltac said softly. "C'mon, kid." He carefully removed the tiny top from the flask. With even more care, he lifted the tiny bottle to Relan's blue and lifeless lips. Only the slightest flutter of air against Boltac's fingers gave him any hope that the lad was still alive. Boltac doubted that there was enough liquid to do more than wet Relan's tongue. There was scarcely a chance that this would work at all. But there was so little chance that any of this should work, so why not? Why not?

He tipped the bottle up and the few drops it contained disappeared into the cave of Relan's mouth. Boltac reached up and grasped his charm necklace. He squeezed all of the many charms so hard they cut into the palm of his hand. Boltac prayed. As the charms cut into his palm and the facets and limbs of the main strange charms filled with his blood, Boltac prayed to everybody.

On the other side of the room, Dimsbury felt the tingle of power dance along his limbs again. The Magic was back! He sat up and exclaimed, "I will have power again." Then he sneezed twice, not understanding the sharp pain that was shooting through his skull. And why did the room look different? Flatter? What was in front of his face? He brought his hand up and bumped something. The pain became excruciating. Dimsbury realized that the Merchant's wand was lodged in his left eye. He collapsed back to the floor with the shock of it and lay there, hyperventilating. He tried to calm himself and think.

With his one good eye he could see what was left of the Flame, the Font of all Magic, guttering and flickering in the circle of jagged spikes that were all that remained of the massive glass jar. The Flame was about to go out. No, thought Dimsbury, this could not be! How could this Merchant–how could this fat, ignorant, money-grubbing aberration–stop a mighty Wizard like Alston Dimsbury? Did he know what a world without Magic would be like? Could such a thing even exist? For himself, and for the greater good, Dimsbury realized he must touch the Flame to restore his power, then somehow coax it back to a fuller life.

As he struggled to regain his feet, a shape appeared before him. Dimsbury looked up and saw Samga. The Orc held his chest with one hand and sagged in pain. Samga said, "Master," because he didn't have another name for the man who lay before him.

"Yes, Samga, my faithful servant after all. Thank goodness I did not strike you down. Please, help me," said the Wizard, not entirely aware that he was begging.

"You made me strong," said Samga.

"Samga, Samga. You are my finest work. All is forgiven, my creation. Bring your father closer to the Flame so that I may regain my power."

Samga bent and picked up Dimsbury.

"Yes, good Samga. Brave Samga," whispered Dimsbury, touching the wand in his eye gingerly.

Samga looked up at the circle of heads mounted on the wall. The broken and aborted things that had led to him. The trial and the error, the arrogant misuse of power in an attempt to craft life itself. Not for the first time, Samga wished that he had never been made.

"Yessss," said Dimsbury. "Just a little closer. Let me dip my fingers in the torrent of Magic and then, and THEN!" Dimsbury was interrupted by a fit of coughing.

As his clacking steps took Samga closer to the flame, he lifted the Wizard high above his head.

"What? What are you doing Samga? Lower me! The Master commands!"

"The Servant does not obey!"

Samga threw the Wizard onto the sharpened teeth of the shattered jar. Dimsbury felt the teeth of glass bite deep into his stomach. Then there was a terrible, tearing noise. The Flame leapt up, again in perfect focus. With perfect hunger, it sucked greedily of Dimsbury's blood. As Dimsbury screamed the flames turned white and leapt up as hungry as any non magical fire had ever been. Dimsbury continued to scream as power shot through him and raked the top of the chamber. The very earth around them shook and still the Wizard screamed.

The Flame folded in on itself. With a crunching of bones and a whimpering, the Wizard was folded up with it. His form flickered in the Magic light, tinier and tinier and tinier, until the Flame shrank to the flicker of a mere candle, and nothing remained of the Wizard.

41

Boltac emerged from the darkness and stood over the tiny Flame. He removed the tattered, burned wool mitten from his hand. For a moment, he considered the struggling Flame. Then he beat it out with three swats.

"mmmmmMMMMMMMM!" protested Asarah. He rushed to her aid and loosened her gag.

"Are you all right?" asked Boltac

"Untie me!"

"En-henh, you're all right. Thank the Gods you're all right. You know, this is a good look for you. Tied up on the ground."

"Boltac, don't ruin this by being cute. Untie me."

"Ruin what?" asked Boltac as he loosened her bonds. "It's already wrecked. I mean seriously, have you looked around you?"

Boltac helped Asarah to her feet, and she threw her arms around him and kissed him. It was a kiss no money could buy, and a kiss that Boltac wouldn't have traded for anything in the world.

"You can say whatever you want, Mr. Boltac, but you came back," she said, kissing him on the nose, "You gave up everything you had to save *me*. That's how I *know*. And that's what makes you a Hero."

"A what? Hero? Don't be silly. I'm not a Hero. I'm just a guy trying to... to..." Boltac realized that he wasn't quite sure who he was anymore, and he liked it that way. "Anyway, if you want a Hero, you should talk to the kid. That's his department, after all. Oh, my Gods, the kid!"

Boltac tore himself from Asarah's arms and rushed to where Relan was slumped against the wall. The Farm Boy still looked like hell, but now his eyes were open. "Did we win?" asked Relan.

"Whattaya mean, did we win?" said Boltac, confused by the question. Then he stood up and looked around. The Wizard was gone. All that remained of the Orcs were now greasy splotches, each with a pile of gold coins in the center. About a stomachful, Boltac thought, before he could banish the terrible thought from his mind. "Henh," said Boltac, letting it really sink in. He walked to the place where Dimsbury had conjured a Magic door to a room full of Treasure. There, in the darkness, stood a perfectly ordinary and unremarkable wooden door.

Boltac pulled the door open. On the other side, Dimsbury's hoard gleamed like a dream of avarice at the end of a cold, dark night.

"We won! We WON!" said Boltac.

"We won," said Relan, as if he didn't believe it. He struggled to get up, and then fell back on the floor with a gasp of pain.

Boltac rushed back to his side. "Easy, kid," said Boltac, "Nobody is more surprised about this than me, but contain your enthusiasm. You're pretty banged up."

"I thought I was dead. I *was* dead. Wasn't I dead? And you said you didn't have any more Magic potions."

"Dead? Kid, there's dead and there's *dead*. Besides, no matter what they tell you, there's always room for negotiation. Even with death."

"Can you stand?" asked Asarah.

"Maybe with some help."

"Then let's get the hell out of here," said Asarah.

Relan grunted and cried out in pain, but eventually he made it to his feet.

"Gah, you're a lug," said Boltac as Relan settled his weight onto their shoulders. The three of them wheeled for the door. But before they could exit the room a dark shape blocked their way. Backlit by the last torch, the terrible form seemed to reach for them. Asarah shrieked. All three of them flinched. But when a second torch blazed to life they could see that it was a trick of the shadows. Samga stood before them, offering them the light.

"You will need it for your journey."

Boltac looked at greasy remains of the other Orcs on the floor and then back to the Orc that stood before him. "Samga, how did you survive?"

"I do not know; I must go to ask the UnderKing."

"Ah, that guy. He'll have an answer, but it won't help you."

"He knows the hidden ways of things," said Samga with a shrug. "He is the only one of my kind that I can speak to."

Boltac took the fabled lamp of Lamptopolis from his belt. It did not light. "Hunh," said Boltac. "Samga, I'm pretty sure this is just a lamp now, but I want you to have it. It's a nice lamp, a quality article. Let it remind you, if you ever need my help, you come. You, I owe."

"But I am a monster. A thing made, not born."

"Ennh, there are monsters and then there are *monsters*," Boltac said with a shrug. "No matter what life hands you, there's always room to negotiate, is what I'm saying."

Boltac took the torch from Samga and they watched as he climbed down into the pit.

They found the main passage and ascended. They stopped to rest several times, but saw and heard nothing in the great expanse of the Wizard's lair. A great underground emptiness surrounded them. The Wizard and his creations were gone.

• • •

Near the exit, they came to a room that was at once familiar and strange. The ceiling had cracked open and now sunlight filled the once-dark room. Here and there around the edge of the room were bones. But the sunlight, the sight of leaves and sky through the ceiling and distant birdsong gave the place a feeling more peaceful than terrible.

In the center of the room there was a dark spot, more dust than anything; in it lay the ornate, jeweled, and cursed mace Boltac had used to trick the Troll what seemed like a lifetime ago.

As Relan and Asarah both gazed at the sunlight and fresh air, Boltac slipped out from underneath Relan's arm and walked to the mace. "Henh," he said. Then he bent down to pick up the cursed mace.

"Don't!" cried Relan weakly, "It's..."

Boltac hefted the mace and turned to Relan. No sinister forces crushed him to the earth. If anything, the mace felt somewhat lighter than before. Boltac said, "Now it's just a blunt instrument." He considered the jewels and ornate carvings that decorated the weapon in his hand. "A faaaancy blunt instrument, but still."

"It's not Magic anymore?" asked Relan.

"Nope. I'm pretty sure not even Magic is Magic anymore," answered Boltac.

"What does that mean?" asked Asarah.

"I dunno," said Boltac, "but I like it."

Boltac lifted Relan, and the three made their awkward way from the dungeon. As they walked into the sunlight of a new day, Boltac thought about all that gold, buried far, far beneath them. "So, uh, kid, you're from a village not far from here, right?"

Relan pointed west with a dejected air, "That way, half a day's walk. Do you know how hard it was for me to get away from there? You're not going to leave me there, are you?"

"No. No?" said Boltac. He looked to Asarah, and she shook her head no. "No. You're with us now. But these villagers, are they uh, big and strong and stupid–I'm sorry, I mean *honest*–like you?"

"Everyone there is the same," Relan sighed, "It is very dull. Why do you want to know?"

"I think I know how to liven it up a bit."

"They don't like outsiders very much."

"Do they like gold? 'Cause if they do, I've got some mining work for them."

"I *really* don't want to go back there."

"Cheer up, it's about to be a very rich village. And you are about to become the Hero you've always wanted to be."

They loaded Relan in the back of the Ducal Coach. Boltac closed the door and stared at the seal of Weeveston Prestidigitous RampartLion Toroble the 15th. "Henh..." he said.

"What?" asked Asarah.

"That's gonna have to change."

42

When he'd seen the large Orc fall to the floor in agony, Rattick had decided it was time to go. Concealed in his cape of fading black, he slunk from the chamber. As he started up the main passageway, he could see flashes and hear crashing noises behind him. He quickened his step and said, "Don't know, don't want to know."

Good thief that he was, it pained Rattick to leave so much gold behind. He was good at taking things, and he enjoyed it. But Rattick was even better at surviving.

By the time the Wizard had started throwing lightning bolts around like they were party favors, Rattick was halfway up the main passage. And just as the walls started shaking, he stepped out into the forest and ran for all he was worth, never looking back.

Rattick couldn't imagine that the Merchant stood a chance against the Wizard, but he couldn't see a percentage in sticking around either way. Rattick had seen Dimsbury lose his temper too often. At the very least, Rattick was certain the guy would unleash his considerable powers to see Robrecht burned to the ground. No, that wouldn't be enough for Dimsbury. He would want to see Robrecht burned to the ground and then its ashes shoveled into the river.

But where there was chaos, thought Rattick, there was opportunity. So when he had escaped the depths, Rattick hid himself away in his favorite tree to see what happened next. What happened next was nothing. Clouds drifted across the sky, and a gentle breeze caused the tree to sway so gently that Rattick fell asleep. As he drifted off, he thought to himself, "No worries, you'll never sleep through the sound of a howling mass of Orcs unleashed on the countryside."

But Rattick awoke to something very, very different. It was the sound of a horse being harnessed. The jingle of metal on metal, the clop of hooves, and the slap of leather. He opened his eyes and realized it was night. The clouds had cleared, and a bright, waxing moon hung in the sky. By its light, he saw Boltac and Asarah help Relan into the Duke's carriage. They had survived? But how?

He watched Boltac and Asarah climb onto the front of the carriage and drive away. Rattick waited many minutes, expecting to hear the howl of bloodthirsty Orcs hurrying in pursuit, or to see fireballs raining down from the heavens upon them. But there was nothing. Nothing at all. Was he dreaming? What was going on?

He descended from the tree and followed them. Of course, he couldn't keep up with a horse-drawn carriage, but the track it left was distinctive enough, and it led back to Robrecht.

He walked through the night, recognizing darkness for the old friend it was. And he had all the small hours of the night to wonder why the cries of Orcs weren't burning up the road behind him.

In the morning, he came upon a small cottage in a clearing. There was smoke rising from the fieldstone chimney. And behind the cottage, in space that was hard-won from the thick, primeval forest, were a garden and a pen with three pigs. Hungry, Rattick made for the garden. As he was rooting around the leafy plants, he heard the door to the cottage open behind him.

In one motion, he swirled his cape of concealment around him and stood stock still in the middle of the garden. He would fool the peasant, he thought, and then resume his free breakfast. What a fine thing to be a thief, and free at the start of a new day.

Peering through a fold in his remarkable cloak, Rattick watched an old man carry the remnants of breakfast to the hogs. The pigs squealed greedily as he filled their trough. The peasant turned and, seeing his garden, he froze.

Rattick remained motionless, wondering what the peasant might be looking at behind him. Then the Peasant asked, "Whattaya doing standing out there in the field? Are ye daft, man? Are ye hurt?"

After a long moment, Rattick unwrapped his cloak and asked, "You can see me?"

"Of course, I can see ya. I may be old and poor, but I'm not blind, am I?"

Rattick stammered. How had the farmer seen him? A master sneak-thief like Rattick, espied by this pie-faced rube?

"If yer simple," the Farmer continued, very slowly, "Follow the road down to Robrecht. There's them that can look after you there." Then the Farmer had a thought, "Or you can stay here and I can hire you as a scarecrow." The Farmer cackled at his own joke as if it was the funniest thing that had ever been said. Rattick hurried away to escape the mocking noise of it.

• • •

When Rattick reached Robrecht, it felt strangely empty. But as he entered through the north gate, the noise of many people gathered drifted to him from the south. At any other time, Rattick would have used a major gathering as a chance to burgle few houses.

Right now, he just had to know what was going on.

43

Rattick slipped into the back of the crowd that was gathered in the courtyard of the old keep. At the center of them all, Boltac stood on a low table, waving his hands for quiet. "C'mon. C'mon, shut up already," he cried.

"Why do you get to be King?" someone demanded. A fine question, thought Rattick: Boltac, King?! How ridiculous would *that* be! Still, he had apparently defeated the Wizard somehow. Rattick had lived so long for two reasons. One, he had no compunctions about killing; two, he was cautious, cautious, cautious. If he didn't understand it, he avoided it. And as he stood there watching a greedy fat man make his appeal, he realized that there was something here he just didn't understand.

It was not a feeling he was comfortable with, by any stretch of his dark and twisted imagination.

Boltac smiled at the man who had questioned his divine right to Kinghood, "I'm glad you asked that question. And there are three reasons. One, 'cause the treasury is bare. That sneaky bastard Weeveston either spent it all or took it with him when he left like a thief in the night." Of course, Boltac meant this as an insult, but Rattick found himself hoping that the former Duke really had been shrewd enough to heist his own Kingdom. That would have been well-played and Rattick would have to remember that trick, if ever he found himself in a similar position.

"But why do you get to be King just because he took the money?" asked another in the crowd.

Rattick didn't like to see what should be a typically surly crowd treating Boltac with anything resembling deference. It disturbed the order of things. Still, that tingle of fear said, you never know who could wind up being a King in these strange days. Always best to err on the side of caution.

"Why? 'Cause I'm going to refill the treasury with my own money. Anybody else want to do that?" The silence was deafening. "Okay, reason #2 why I should be your King is that, effective immediately, I'm cutting taxes," Boltac shook his head. It hurt him to say the next words, but desperate times called for desperate measures, "in half."

A cheer went up, but the naturally skeptical Robrecht crowd still wasn't totally with him. They had heard too many lies about taxes in their days. Boltac didn't hesitate.

"And reason number three. At this very moment, the forces of the Mercian Empire–of which we were so recently a protectorate–are on their way to reclaim us. By force, even if that's not even a little bit necessary. Because that's the way people think when they are part of an Empire."

"That's not a reason to make you King. That's a reason to surrender!" said a fat man in the front.

"En-henh. I'm not too sure they're gonna take 'uncle' for an answer, if you know what I'm saying. No, they're gonna be plenty pissed and looking for someone to blame. And if I know my Mercian tactics, they are going to come stomping in here looking for someone to make an example of."

"Well, then the Horks, surely. They'll take it out on the Horks."

"Yeah, but I told you: no more Horks. Orcs. Whatever. I took care of them."

Relan jumped up on the table next to Boltac. Rattick could see, before the lad even opened his mouth, that the crowd was ready to believe him. The thief shook his head. You just couldn't fake that kind of innocence and naiveté. If Rattick could fake *that*, he'd be a much wealthier man by now. "I can vouch for his story," said Relan, "I was there. And what's more, this man saved my life."

Boltac didn't waste the opportunity. "Anyone woulda done the same," said Boltac, playing to the crowd. "But the thing is, not finding any Orcs, the Mercians are gonna say it was a hoax. A revolt of some kind. And they will want to take out their frustration by cracking some heads open. And since the only heads here are ours, well, friends, something should be done."

Affirmative cries rose from the crowd. Yeah! Something should be done!

"Anybody got a plan?" Boltac asked, dead earnest.

"But *you're* supposed to have a plan. You're the King!"

"Oh, am I?"

There was a grumbling in the crowd. Rattick thought Boltac was going to falter. But he saw Boltac look to a balcony high on the keep behind him. There, in the sunlight and clean air, was Asarah, as radiant as spring. She smiled and waved her palms in a motion that said 'keep calm.'

Boltac turned back and smiled at the crowd, armed with new confidence. "So, here's the deal. I have a plan, and if I'm your King, I'll use it. If any of *you* have a plan, well then, you can put your own money in the treasury, face not only the wrath of the most powerful Empire in the Four Kingdoms but also the ire of your fellow citizens... you know, come to think of it, I don't want this after all." In a display of master showmanship, Boltac jumped off the table. "Nah, I'm taking my plan and going home."

"No, no, no!" rose the cries around him. The negotiation successfully concluded; Boltac climbed back onto the table and smiled.

"Okay, here's what we are going to do..." And Boltac told them the plan.

And through all of it, Asarah beamed down on him like an angel.

"Wait just a minute," said an old man, missing a few teeth said slowly. "If you're to be King, don't you need a coronation first?"

"Ahh. Maybe it'd be best to wait until after I've saved my new Kingdom, hunh?"

Nobody argued.

And with that, Rattick decided that the jig was up. He spent the night in a house of questionable virtue and reasonable rates. And when he cinched up his pants the next morning, he was certain it was the last time he would ever see Robrecht.

Later, as he drifted down the river Swift in a stolen boat, he was also certain Robrecht would never see Boltac's coronation either. Doubted the dismal, foggy burg would last much longer. And he couldn't say that he was going to miss it.

44

Weeveston Prestidigitous RampartLion Toroble the 15th stumbled out onto the stone terrace and flung himself down on a divan. Down the terraced hill, he could see the slow-moving remnants of the river Swift. Here in the Southron lands, the name and character of the river had changed completely. Weeveston smiled to himself without knowing why. But he didn't need a reason. He was still pleasantly drunk from a night of revelry that had not yet ended.

On the other side of the river, the pure, clean, hopeful light of a new day had made its way through the twisted streets and high towers of the fabled Scented City of Shatnapur. By the time these rays of dawn had reached Weeveston, they had fewer illusions and far less purity. Still, the miasma of incense and highly cultivated vice rising from the city towers tinged the light a pleasant shade of red.

There was the pad of a sandaled foot on the flagstones behind him. He turned and smiled at his wife Tryphaenae, who was a vision of beauty in the corrupted light of dawn.

"I have ordered the servants to bring us breakfast," said Tryphaenae as she sat next to him with flounce of bangles and jewelry.

"Ah, my darling, you shouldn't strain yourself so, making breakfast for me."

Tryphaenae smiled. "Ordering breakfast is the least I can do for your return, my loving husband."

"And what is the most you might do?" Weeveston said lewdly. Tryphaenae turned to avoid his grope so he could not see the look of distaste on her face.

She removed herself to another couch and said, "Save your strength, Weeveston."

Then a train of servants emerged with the first course of breakfast. As Weeveston lay back and let himself be waited on, he thought, this is what I was born to be.

There was a tremendous pounding at the door. Weeveston finished sucking the contents of a poached sparrow egg and said, "My dear, are you conducting renovations?"

Tryphaenae shook her head. "No, Weeveston."

The pounding continued, this time even louder.

"I say, is that your, I mean *our*, front door?"

"I believe it might be. But why the pounding? It is unlocked." The pounding was replaced with a commotion inside the house. Weeveston saw the glint of highly polished armor before he recognized who it was walking out onto the terrace.

"Uncle Torvalds," said Weeveston, "Why, you are just in time for breakfast."

"My breakfast was three hours ago," barked Torvalds.

Weeveston continued, "And a good morning to you too, Uncle. Are you sure you wouldn't care for some toast? Or whatever passes for toast here in the south–you do have toast here, my darling? You remember my wife Tryphaenae, Uncle?"

"I arranged the marriage," growled Torvalds. He turned to the nearest servant and commanded, "Have a horse saddled for my nephew." Torvalds tone was such that the servant didn't even look to the mistress of the house before he ran off.

Torvalds turned his attention to his niece-by-marriage. "Ah, my dear Tryphaenae, you are as lovely as the day you were married."

From her divan, Tryphaenae smiled. "Torvalds, you old rogue."

He bowed. "Guilty as charged. I am sorry that I must take him away from you so soon after you have been reunited, but the affairs of state..."

Tryphaenae smiled invitingly and said, "I have always been *very* understanding when it comes to affairs. Do what you will."

Torvalds kissed her hand and said, "Our time together is always so brief, my dear." Then the smile dropped away from his face and he turned back to his nephew.

"You have lost a Kingdom–"

"Duchy?" offered Weeveston.

"–and we take our army to win it back."

"Army?" asked Weeveston. "What army? I thought all of our forces were far, far to the north?"

"I have hired the Free Companions. All of them. At present they are marching north. We ride to join them and retake your throne."

Weeveston did not get up.

"Time is of the essence," Torvalds said through clenched teeth.

"That's it? Hired an army and off we go? No 'hello,' no 'how are you'? No 'glad to see you'? No niceties at all, Uncle? No concern for your poor nephew, driven from his seat by an army of creatures most foul. Horks, as they are called in the benighted regions of my former Kingdom."

"Duchy," corrected Torvalds "Let's go."

Weeveston, with uncharacteristic courage, sat his ground.

Torvalds sighed. "Nephew. I am not glad to see you. Your debacle has torn me from pressing business in the west. I should think it enough that I am here to help you fix your problem and restore you to the function and station to which your family has so graciously appointed you. However, if you require a reminder of the warm embrace of family which is denied to you due to your own obvious shortcomings, then I will tell you that your Aunt sends her best."

Weeveston jumped and checked behind him for a highly skilled assassin. Finding himself not murdered, he rose and said, "Yes, yes. Posthaste, Uncle, as you say."

•   •   •

Within two days, they joined the main body of the Free Companions, an army-for-hire 20,000 strong. The men were open and easy with each other and their commanders. Their laughter and song on the march provided a fine counterpoint to grim Uncle Torvalds and the detachment of Mercian BattleMages with him.

Even on a good day, a BattleMage was an odd sort of duck. Weeveston couldn't remember a Wizard who wasn't, in one way or another, but the four that his uncle had brought seemed particularly humorless. Still, they did their job. The threat of their sinister Magic kept the Free Companions civil. Really, thought Weeveston, mercenaries? Not a very good idea. How could one trust a mercenary? How could one trust anyone, for that matter, thought Weeveston.

As he considered this, the leader of the Free Companions—a swarthy, long-haired man known as Laughlin—turned in his saddle and looked at him. Weeveston found it disconcerting and gave the man a nervous little grin. Laughlin smiled broadly revealing several gold teeth. Then he turned forward again and laughed a booming laugh. His long black hair was bound with a red scarf—the mark of the Free Companions—and Weeveston could see it shaking with laughter long after he could no longer hear the sound.

Weeveston shivered. He did not like these *Companions*. They showed no rank or discipline. They had no uniforms. All that was required of them was that they display some red piece of armor or apparel. Laughlin had boasted it was so they would be easier to find. And these crass braggarts were feared fighters? Weeveston was not a warlike man, but he could not understand it. These were men you could only trust while winning. His uncle always won. But against Horks?

The column continued the northward march for a week and a half. When the river Swift was not lost in deep gorges and defiles, they traveled the road beside it. And in its rapids and falls, Weeveston often thought he could hear mocking laughter.

When he left Robrecht the last time, he had really believed he'd gotten out from under. But it seemed the world did not work that way. No, a man couldn't change his station just because he wanted to. So Weeveston was being dragged to a reunion with his destiny already in progress. A damn damp destiny in a dank castle at the center of a dull town. Weeveston blinked back a few tears as he thought about it.

His self-pity was interrupted by a commotion from further up the road. He heard the cries of "Scout! Scout!" and spurred his horse to reach his uncle in the vanguard. From a distance he could see his dour uncle perk up. Weeveston got there the same time as a rider on a lathered horse. Torvalds demanded, "Have you sighted them? How many are there? How are they armed? What is their disposition?"

"One, my Lord."

"One?" snorted Torvalds, "One what?"

"One carriage approaches my Lord, flying a banner of truce."

"Oh. Oh, well, let them through. This may be easier than I thought." The word went up the ranks and, with some grumbling, the Free Companions parted so a white carriage could reach them. Torvalds and Weeveston dismounted and prepared to receive the parley.

"I say," said Weeveston, "I think that's my carriage."

The young blonde lad who drove the carriage handled the reins smartly. As he wheeled the coach to a stop, all eyes were on the carriage door. For a moment, nothing happened. From inside the carriage, a muffled voice commanded, "Say it!"

"Oh, right," said the driver. "Sorry." He looked at Weeveston and Torvalds and said, "Sorry, I'm new at this. We both are."

"Don't apologize, just say it already!" said the voice from inside the carriage.

The driver sat up straighter and said, "Boltac the Shrewd, King of Robrecht, first of his name."

The door swung open and Boltac waddled out.

"Hello," said Boltac, "You must be the guy in charge," he said to Torvalds, "'cause you look pissed."

"You have stolen our Duchy," said Torvalds.

"Stolen? I haven't stolen anything. He"–Boltac pointed at Weeveston– "ran away. Besides," he said with a smile, "it ain't a Duchy. It's a Kingdom. And I'm the King."

"You are no King. You are not even of a royal line,"

"Whattaya mean I'm not the King of Robrecht? I rode here in the King's carriage!"

"That's my ducal carriage!" Weeveston protested.

"No. It used to be. Look, the seal is changed and everything." Boltac looked directly at Torvalds and said, "I drove your idiot nephew out and took his carriage and his castle and his town back for the people of Robrecht. You're not welcome anymore."

Weeveston peered at the new sigil. "What is that? A fish?"

Boltac said, "It's an Eelpout. It's like a fish's ugly cousin. And you see those words?"

Weeveston read as if it was difficult for him, "'Everybody pays their way'? What kind of motto is that?"

"This foolishness changes nothing," said Torvalds. "It is our Duchy and we have the army with which prove it." With a wave of his hand he indicated Laughlin on his tall horse, grinning through his beard at the proceedings. Torvalds pointed to a few of the Companions and said, "You! Seize him!"

None of the Companions moved.

"En-henh, about that," said Boltac.

"Seize him!" Torvalds said, stamping his foot at the Companions' impudence.

"I don't know *why* they call them the *Free* Companions. 'Cause we both know they don't come cheap," said Boltac with a smile.

"You are using the gold from our own treasury to hire an army to fight us! SUCH IMPUDENCE! I will drag your body through the streets behind my own horse!"

"En-henh," said Boltac, "So, funny thing about *that*. There was no gold in the treasury. It was all gone. Robrecht was broke. I can't say I was surprised, seeing how your boy here saw fit to loot our fair city six ways from Sunday. So I refilled the treasury on my own."

"What? How?"

"Yeah, see, this is why the call me the Hero of Robrecht. This is why they made me King. I bought it. Just like I bought your army."

"They would never turn against us. Then they would never be safe against the Feared BattleMages of Mercia." Torvalds gave the phrase all of the ominous gravity he could manage. A low, nervous murmur rippled through the crowd of mercenaries that surrounded them. It was true, they were frightened of Magic. Boltac had told Laughlin that he could take care of the BattleMages–that was part of the deal– but these hard men could not understand how one fat Merchant could handle the powerful Mages when they could not.

Boltac didn't miss a beat. "Okay, so funny thing about *BattleMages*. Well, hang on. You got one of them fancy BattleMages lying around? I'll just show you."

Within moments, the four sinister, tattooed men came to the center of the circle. The tallest of them looked down at Boltac and sneered,

"What do you think, brothers? Should I transmogrify this one into a pig, or is he already pig enough?" The BattleMages laughed humorlessly at their leader's joke-like object.

Boltac chuckled along with them and then grew serious, "I don't think you could mans-trog-mify your ass with both hands."

"YOU DARE TO—" But before the Chief BattleMage could vent his full fury, Boltac walked over and slapped him across the face. The slap made a sharp noise that carried well. Everyone gasped in amazement. Even Torvalds.

"Yeah, I dare plenty. Now strike me down. Or pull a rabbit out of a hat. I don't care. Just work some Magic already."

The Mage raised his hands in the air and began a guttural chant that rose in volume and intensity. His eyes rolled back into his head. Even as the crowd parted behind Boltac, the Merchant stood his ground. As the Mage reached a full-throated yell, he whipped his entire body and threw his hands at Boltac.

The BattleMage held this pose for a moment, but nothing happened. Then shook his hands in frustration. Then looked at the tips of his fingers. A blush covered his face and overwhelmed the red handprint where Boltac had slapped him.

"En-henh. Nuttin." Boltac turned to the crowd and said, "See? They're frauds. FRAUDS! Their Magic doesn't work anymore."

Torvalds, with fear in his voice, turned to the Mages and said, "But you told me it was just that the portents were bad. That it was an 'ill-omened time for the working of great Magicks'!"

With that the crowd burst into laughter. There were hoots and howls of derision. One of the men even threw a clod of earth and hit the BattleMage in the face.

"All right! All right!" yelled Boltac, waving his arms for quiet. None of the men listened, but their commander, Laughlin, dismounted and strode to the center of the gathering. He did not even have to speak. He raised his large, gloved hand and the men fell silent. He looked to Boltac and asked, "Are we through?"

"A few more words," said Boltac.

"Traitor," Torvalds hissed at Laughlin. "You have lost any chance you had to become a full citizen of the Mercian Empire."

Laughlin smiled and stepped out from between Boltac and Torvalds.

"So, Torvalds. There's no reason this has to get ugly. Mostly because I didn't hire these exorbitantly priced Companions to fight you." Boltac nodded at Laughlin who now stood in the circle behind Torvalds. "That's a compliment, you're a hell of a negotiator."

Boltac continued, "I hired them NOT to fight you. Less risk. Cheaper that way. In fact, I made them all citizens. Gave them each a nice plot of land, reclaiming an area that had been recently terrorized by an Evil Wizard and his creations."

Weeveston asked, "What happened to the Wizard? What have you done with Dimsbury?"

"Ennh, Magic was a dangerous business while it lasted. But, here's the thing. Just 'cause I'm not paying these guys, doesn't mean they can't rip you limb from limb for their own enjoyment."

The men cheered.

"So, I suggest you turn around and walk back the way you came as quickly as possible. You could even run."

Deeply affronted, Torvalds exclaimed, "You are stealing our horses?"

"Oh, no, Kings don't steal. Kings *never* steal. Your horses have either been commandeered. Or appropriated. But stolen, don't be ridiculous."

"You are a vile little man!" said Torvalds

"Your Highness," said Boltac.

"What?" sputtered Torvalds.

"'You are a vile little man, your *Highness*.' You forgot to add 'your Highness'. Very bad to do this when addressing a King."

"Enough of this madness!" Torvalds drew his sword, lifting it for a swing that would surely have cleaved Boltac in two. But before the sword could start forward, a foot of steel emerged from Torvalds' belly. Behind him, Laughlin put his knee on Torvalds' Shining™ Armor and recovered his dirk. Blood sputtered from Torvalds' lips as he collapsed to his knees. He fell to the ground at Boltac's feet. Weeveston looked on in wide-eyed horror.

"What a waste," said Boltac shaking his head. Then he put a sympathetic hand on Weeveston's shoulder and walked him away, "You don't need to look at that, trust me."

As they walked south Boltac said, "Look, Weeveston, if that's even your real name, we've got easily defensible mountain passes. We're on the trade road to everywhere. And now we've got our own Kingdom. We'd like to be friends with everybody, you understand. Friends and trading partners. 'Cause it's good for business. Anger, bad blood, ancient feuds–all of that garbage is bad for business, right? So, before I let you go, I gotta know. Do you want to be my friend?"

Pale and shaking, Weeveston looked behind him. Laughlin was wiping Uncle Torvalds blood from his dirk. He smiled again.

"I do. I do want to be friends," Weeveston said, looking around nervously.

"I do want to be friends, what?"

"What?" asked Weeveston, truly not understanding.

"No. Not what. What do you say?"

"Oh, I do want to be friends, your H-h-h-highness?"

"Okay then. Shake hands and run along."

"I'm not sure you are supposed to shake hands with a King."

"Don't be silly, I'm not that kind of King."

Boltac shook Weeveston's soft hand and watched him scurry south as fast as his expensive shoes would allow. From beside him, Boltac heard Laughlin chuckle. The big man made a clicking noise with his tongue as he shook his head.

"You know they will come for you," said Laughlin.

"En-henh," said Boltac. He looked at Laughlin and said, "And you know they're gonna to come for you too."

Laughlin smiled again. A smile that had survived a countless fights and endless miles of contested ground. He shrugged and said, "It will be expensive for them, either way."

"En-henh," said Boltac.

45

Rattick leered at the serving boy who writhed through the crowded, smoke filled-room. Then he threw him a coin and motioned for another bottle of wine. He raised his half-empty glass in a silent toast to the unlucky man whose stolen purse was funding his party. Fate might have reduced him to a simple cutpurse, but so far, his new station was treating him well.

Rattick never saw it coming. He didn't hear the thock of the leather-covered sap that hit him across the back of his head. He never felt the rough hands that deposited him in the back of the wagon. He was unaware of the hard gallop north.

When he awoke, the first thing he was aware of was a tremendous headache. He opened his eyes and saw that he was in the back of a canvas-covered wagon. Rattick wondered where the serving boy had gone. Then he wondered where the inn had gone. When he saw fog blowing through the gaps in the canvas he wondered where the entire city of Shatnapur had gone. A chill came over him. The cold. The fog. That's when he knew he was headed back to Robrecht.

He attempted to roll over and discovered that he was bound hand and foot. He struggled and shouted, but nothing came of it, so he gave up and went back to sleep. The next time he awoke it was to the sound of horse hooves ringing on cobblestones. He was taken from the back of the wagon like a sack of grain and deposited in front of a stable. One of his captors, a swarthy man who flashed gold teeth at Rattick when he smiled, cut him free with a well-used dirk.

The man said, "Wash yourself. You are to appear before the King."

"King?" ask Rattick. He surveyed the courtyard of Robrecht's central keep. "This isn't a Kingdom."

The man in the bandanna cuffed him across the mouth and said, "Don't speak ill of your King. One might get the idea that you're a traitor." The he laughed, flashing his gold teeth again. Rattick licked the raw place the cuff left on his mouth. He estimated how much he would sell this man's gold teeth for after he had killed him.

But not yet. First he must figure out what was going on here. Then somehow win his freedom. Then insinuate himself into this soldier's confidence. Then betray him. Slip the knife in when he least expected it. A few sharp jerks with a pair of pliers and then away.

But what was going on here? He saw more fighters coming and going in the courtyard. That would suggest that Robrecht had been overrun. The place should have been raped and pillaged out of existence by now. But the city was strangely intact.

"Clean yourself," the man in the bandanna said again, prodding him towards the water in the horse trough.

Rattick rubbed his jaw with the cold water in the basin to ease the sting of the rising bruise. Then he washed himself as best he could. Before he could finish, two soldiers had grabbed him by the arms and hauled him into the castle. Doors, rooms, hallways, all passed in a blur until finally Rattick was thrown onto the floor of a large room. Behind him, he heard a man say, "Rattick, a man not to be trusted." Rattick turned and saw a man in formal dress holding himself perfectly erect. The man did not return Rattick's gaze, but instead looked unwaveringly toward the front of the room.

When Rattick followed the Chamberlain's gaze, he saw Boltac standing before the throne, wearing something that looked like a crown. "Ha," Rattick said.

"You should have more respect when addressing the King," someone said from off to the side. He turned his head to the left and there was Relan, dressed in fine clothing and wearing a polished breastplate that featured a rampant... eelpout? What in the hell was going on here?

"I thought I killed you. I'm sure I killed you," said Rattick.

"En-henh, maybe you're slipping in your old age Rattick. Maybe it's time you considered a new line of work."

"While the loss would wound me deeply, how is it that you are not dead? Why has the Empire seen fit to let a Merchant play Kinglet with its property."

"Because I'm cunning and I know how to buy things cheap. Any more questions?"

"And how is it I am not dead?"

Boltac rolled his head to one side and squinted. "From the look of it, I'd say you're not dead because you've got a very thick skull. That and I've got a proposition for you."

"A proposition," Rattick said, getting to his feet.

"Well, Rattick, it's like this," Boltac said. "Turns out, I'm a King after all."

"Ha," said Rattick.

"I know, no one is more surprised than I am. But here we are and the only thing to do is make the best of it. So, I'd like to make you my first Minister."

"What! This snake? He would not be a Good and Loyal Minister," protested Relan.

"Exactly. Precisely. Just when I think you are hopeless, kid, you show a glimmer of real intelligence."

"You could never trust him," said Relan.

"You *could* trust your loyal and humble servant," said Rattick, bowing low and glaring at Relan.

"See, that's just it. I'm not going to trust him. That's where everybody goes wrong in this King game. They start trusting their advisors and then bango, they are betrayed. And they wind up with their heads on pikes and confused looks on their faces as the crows peck out their eyeballs.

"I don't want to trust him. I want him to try everything he possibly can. If I'm safe against my 'friends', I will certainly be safe against my enemies."

"My Lord, I am at your service," said Rattick as he bowed even lower this time.

"Skip the sarcasm, Rattick. I'm a King now, so it's not Lord. It's Your Highness."

"King Boltac?" Rattick asked.

"What did I just tell you about the sarcasm? See Relan? Do you see what a wonderful Disloyal Minister he makes? Now come here, Rattick; kneel so you can receive your badge of office."

"You mean you are not going to have me killed? You really mean to do this? Appoint me as Minister to your court?"

"Disloyal Minister. Minister of Disloyalty and Sedition. We can work out the title later, but yes, yeah, you slippery bastard. I want you where I can keep an eye on you."

Rattick knelt and said, "This is going to be a very different sort of Kingdom, my liege." This time there was not the slightest hint of sarcasm in his voice.

"Yes, it is. There's no Magic anymore, Rattick. So who knows where the progress will stop." Then Boltac draped a robe of office around Rattick's shoulders.

Rattick said, "Progress is Magic, my liege."

"Well spoken, Rattick. Although I distrust your flattery."

"You are right to do so, my liege."

"Now, arise, my Disloyal Minister. You have the run of the keep. But if you try to leave and get caught, you'll be killed. So either stick around or be really sneaky. Preferably both."

"Sire, my first advice as Minister is to be rid of this peasant. This ox is more useful to you as a martyr than as a, a, a, what is he? Errand boy? Valet?""

"Why just look at him Rattick. He's the Hero, anybody can see that."

"Hero? How can he be the Hero? He's not even a Knight."

"Excellent point, Rattick!" Boltac turned to Relan, "See how useful this guy is?"

"He is a bad man," said Relan.

"You think you rule a Kingdom by being Mr. Nice Guy all the time? Now get over here and take a knee, so I can Knight you."

"A Knight? How can I be a Knight? Don't I have to be a squire first?"

Boltac smiled at the Farm Boy, still so innocent in the ways of the world, and oblivious to what had happened, "I'm a King, and I didn't have to be a Prince first.

"But I don't know anything about being a Knight!"

"I don't know anything about being a King, so we'll both figure it out as we go along."

"I don't think this is a very good idea. I'm really not comfortable–"

"En-henh," said Boltac, "So you know the first rule of being a Knight?"

"No, see, I don't even know what the first rule is!"

"The first rule is you obey the King."

"Right," Relan nodded. "Obey the King."

"Now kneel and hold still so I can knight you."

"To Knight him you need a sword," said Rattick, "Shall I go get a blade for you?"

"Wrong again, Rattick. You are a natural at this job. No swords. No more disguising a fancy club by calling it a scepter." Boltac picked up an ornate scale from a stand beside the throne. Boltac carefully touched Relan on one shoulder and then the next. Then he said, "Deal fairly with all. Now arise, Sir Relan, first Knight of Robrecht."

"But..." protested Relan.

"Obey!" said the King. After Relan stood Boltac said, "Congratulations, the both of you. Sir Relan, I expect great things from you. Minister, I expect horrible things from you. The good and the bad. Now get outta here. Both of you. You too, Chamberlain. No more visitors. Court's closed."

As they left the room Asarah entered.

Boltac smiled at her and asked, "And where have you been?"

"Well, my liege," she said with a playful curtsy, "I have been surveying our new home. And I have learned something very important about it. It is very damp."

"Damp?"

"Damp. Moisture from the river seems to creep up the stones. This place is frightfully clammy. If I didn't know better, I would say that it was enchanted. Cursed even."

"So, it just needs a good airing out, maybe?"

Asarah laughed. "Oh, no. No, no, no. This place is not homey at all. It will not do. Drafty, damp, strong-looking on the outside but in no way impressive or refined. Perhaps it is enough for a second-rate Duke, but for a King..." She tsked. "It will not do. We must build you a castle, my liege."

Boltac sighed. All of a sudden he felt very tired. Everyone turning to him, asking what should be done. Always more questions, more problems and fewer answers. Was he even doing any of this right? Was this what being a King was all about? Now that he had time to think about it, he wondered if he'd ever get the hang of it.

He walked over to the wooden throne and sat down on it heavily. "Ennh," he said, listening to the creaking and feeling the sharp edges of the chair bite into his legs. "This chair is not a quality item."

"Well, have another one made." She took his hand and nodded encouragingly at him. "After all, you are a King now. You get to have things the way you want them."

"If we have to build a new castle, I'm not sure I can afford things the way I want them."

She kissed him on the cheek and said, "Don't be cheap. It's unbecoming of your station."

"Enh-henh," he said. Then he kissed her and, for a moment, forgot all the worries of being a King.

Now What?

If you liked this book, the kindest thing you can do for the author is to tell a friend, or even a stranger about it. Why not write a review on amazon or goodreads?

Also, if you join my email list[1] You'll get access to all kinds of wonderful things, including a lovely pdf of *Boltac's Mercantile Guide to Better Living through Sharp Trading*. So sign up. It may be the only time a fictional character can teach you something that will save you a couple of bucks.

www.patrickemclean.com

---

[1]www.patrickemclean.com/merchantsignup

The World's Most Dangerous About the Author Blurb.

You know those "About the Author" blurbs that begin with poignant details from the writer's childhood? The ones that quickly move through a series of credentials and accomplishments so impressive that they make you feel that if you don't buy a book, everyone will recognize you for the uncultured Phillistine [2] that you are? Yeah, this is not that kind of author blurb. This is the other kind.

This is an About the Author blurb that actually tells you about the author. If you stick with this blurb it will tell you that Patrick has been shot, has fallen off a mountain, was once framed for a crime he did not commit — that he has gambled with his rent money and knows how to replace the water pump in a 1966 Chrysler. It will also explain to you that, much like a lost boy raised by wolves, he was brought up by economists and can interpret the strange dances and guttural utterances of their dismal tribe. But most of all this blurb wants you to know that Patrick can write. That he puts words and concepts and characters together in a way that will make your synapses light up like an accident in an unlicensed fireworks factory. Yes, a substance that powerful should be made illegal. But before that happens, you've got a chance to go to www.patrickemclean.com to get more of his writing.

If you don't use this chance, Patrick won't hold it against you. After all, he's a nice, easy-going kind of guy. But this Blurb will know.

---

[2] Editor's Note – Patrick put an extra l in Phillistine here just to make sure it STAYED down. Don't let him fool you. He's also a little dangerous. Especially with a consonant close to hand.

And believe me, this is one "About the Author" blurb you don't want to cross.